NO LONGER HUMAN

ALSO BY OSAMU DAZAI

THE SETTING SUN

NO LONGER HUMAN

BY OSAMU DAZAI

TRANSLATED BY DONALD KEENE

A NEW DIRECTIONS BOOK

First published clothbound by New Directions in 1958
First published as New Directions Paperbook 357 in 1973

Manufactured in the United States of America

New Directions Books are published for James Laughlin
by New Directions Publishing Corporation
80 Eighth Avenue, New York 10011

30 29 28 27

This translation is dedicated with affection
to Nancy and Edmundo Lassalle

TRANSLATOR'S INTRODUCTION

I think that Osamu Dazai would have been gratified by the reviews his novel *The Setting Sun* received when the English translation was published in the United States. Even though some of the critics were distressed by the picture the book drew of contemporary Japan, they one and all discussed it in the terms reserved for works of importance. There was no trace of the condescension often bestowed on writings emanating from remote parts of the world, and for once nobody thought to use the damning adjective "exquisite" about an unquestionably Japanese product. It was judged among its peers, the moving and beautiful books of the present generation.

3

One aspect of *The Setting Sun* puzzled many readers, however, and may puzzle others in Dazai's second novel *No Longer Human*:[1] the role of Western culture in Japanese life today. Like Yozo, the chief figure of *No Longer Human*, Dazai grew up in a small town in the remote north of Japan, and we might have expected his novels to be marked by the simplicity, love of nature and purity of sentiments of the inhabitants of such a place. However, Dazai's family was rich and educated, and from his childhood days he was familiar with European literature, American movies, reproductions of modern paintings and sculpture and much else of our civilization. These became such important parts of his own experience that he could not help being influenced by them, and he mentioned them quite as freely as might any author in Europe or America. In reading his works, however, we are sometimes made aware that Dazai's understanding or use of these elements of the West is not always the same as ours. It is easy to conclude from this that Dazai had only half digested them, or even that the Japanese as a whole have somehow misappropriated our culture.

I confess that I find this parochialism curious in the United States. Here where our suburbs are

[1] The literal translation of the original title *Ningen Shikkaku* is "Disqualified as a Human Being." I have elsewhere referred to this same novel as "The Disqualified."

jammed with a variety of architecture which bears no relation to the antecedents of either the builders or the dwellers; where white people sing Negro spirituals and a Negro soprano sings Lucia di Lammermoor at the Metropolitan Opera; where our celebrated national dishes, the frankfurter, the hamburger and chow mein betray by their very names non-American origins: can we with honesty rebuke the Japanese for a lack of purity in their modern culture? And can we criticize them for borrowing from us, when we are almost as conspicuously in their debt? We find it normal that we drink tea, their beverage, but curious that they should drink whiskey, ours. Our professional decorators, without thinking to impart to us an adequate background in Japanese aesthetics, decree that we should brighten our rooms with Buddhist statuary or with lamps in the shapes of paper-lanterns. Yet we are apt to find it incongruous if a Japanese ornaments his room with examples of Christian religious art or a lamp of Venetian glass. Why does it seem so strange that another country should have a culture as conglomerate as our own?

There are, it is true, works of recent Japanese literature which are relatively untouched by Western influence. Some of them are splendidly written, and convince us that we are getting from them what is most typically Japanese in modern fiction. If, however, we do not wish to resemble the Frenchman who finds the detective story the only worthwhile part of American literature, we must also be willing to read Japanese novels in which a modern (by modern I mean Western) intelligence is at work.

A writer with such an intelligence—Dazai was one —may also be attracted to the Japanese traditional culture, but it will virtually be with the eyes of a foreigner who finds it appealing but remote. Dostoievski and Proust are much closer to him than any Japanese writer of, say, the eighteenth century. Yet we should be unfair to consider such a writer a cultural *déraciné*; he is not much farther removed from his eighteenth century, after all, than we are from ours. In his case, to be sure, a foreign culture has intervened, but that culture is now in its third generation in Japan. No Japanese thinks of his business suit as an outlandish or affected garb; it is not only what he normally wears, but was probably also the costume of his father and grandfather before him. To wear Japanese garments would actually be strange and uncomfortable for most men. The majority of Japanese of today wear modern Western culture also as they wear their clothes, and to keep reminding them that their ancestors originally attired themselves otherwise is at once bad manners and foolish.

It may be wondered at the same time if the

Japanese knowledge of the West is more than a set of clothes, however long worn or well tailored. Only a psychologist could properly attempt to answer so complex a question, although innumerable casual visitors to Japan have readily opined that under the foreign exterior the Japanese remain entirely unlike ourselves. I find this view hard to accept. It is true that the Japanese of today differ from Americans— perhaps not more, however, than do Greeks or Portuguese—but they are certainly much more like Americans than they are like their ancestors of one hundred years ago. As far as literature is concerned, the break with the Japanese past is almost complete.

In Japanese universities today the Japanese literature department is invariably one of the smallest and least supported. The bright young men generally devote themselves to a study of Western institutions or literature, and the academic journals are filled with learned articles on the symbolism of Leconte de Lisle or on the correspondence of James Knox Polk. The fact that these articles will never be read abroad, not even by specialists in Leconte de Lisle or James Knox Polk, inevitably creates a sense of isolation and even loneliness among intellectuals. Some Japanese of late have taken to referring to themselves as "the orphans of Asia," indicating (and perhaps lamenting) the fact that although Japan has become isolated from the rest of Asia, the Western nations do not accept her literature or learning as part of their own. The Japanese writers of today are cut off from Asian literature as completely as the United States is from Latin American literature, by the conviction that there is nothing to learn. This attitude may be mistaken, but I remember how shocked a Japanese novelist, a friend of mine, was to see his own name included on a list of Lebanese, Iraqi, Burmese and miscellaneous other Asian writers who had been sponsored by an American foundation. He would undoubtedly have preferred to figure at the tail end of a list of Western writers or of world writers in general than to be classed with such obscure exotics.

We might like to reprimand the Japanese for the neglect of their own traditional culture, or to insist that Japanese writers should be proud to be associated with other Asians, but such advice comes too late: as the result of our repeated and forcible intrusions in the past, Western tastes are coming to dominate letters everywhere. The most we have reason to expect in the future are world variants of a single literature, of the kind which already exist nationally in Europe.

No Longer Human is almost symbolic of the predicament of the Japanese writers today. It is the story of a man who is orphaned from his fellows by their refusal to take him seriously. He is denied the love of his father, taken advantage of by his friends, and finally in turn is cruel to the women who love him. He does not insist because of his experiences that the others are all wrong and he alone right. On the contrary, he records with devastating honesty his every transgression of a code of human conduct which he cannot fathom. Yet, as Dazai realized (if the "I" of the novel did not), the cowardly acts and moments of abject collapse do not tell the whole story. In a superb epilogue the only objective witness testifies, "He was an angel," and we are suddenly made to realize the incompleteness of Yozo's portrait of himself. In the way that most men fail to see their own cruelty, Yozo had not noticed his gentleness and his capacity for love.

Yozo's experiences are certainly not typical of all Japanese intellectuals, but the sense of isolation which they feel between themselves and the rest of the world is perhaps akin to Yozo's conviction that he alone is not "human." Again, his frustrations at the university, his unhappy involvement with the Communist Party, his disastrous love affairs, all belong to the past of many writers of today. At the same time, detail after detail clearly is derived from the individual experience of Osamu Dazai himself. The temptation is strong to consider the book as a barely fictionalized autobiography, but this would be a mistake, I am sure. Dazai had the creative artistry of a great cameraman. His lens is often trained on moments of his own past, but thanks to his brilliant skill in composition and selection his photographs are not what we expect to find cluttering an album. There is nothing of the meandering reminiscer about Dazai; with him all is sharp, brief and evocative. Even if each scene of *No Longer Human* were the exact reproduction of an incident from Dazai's life— of course this is not the case—his technique would qualify the whole of the work as one of original fiction.

No Longer Human is not a cheerful book, yet its effect is far from that of a painful wound gratuitously inflicted on the reader. As a reviewer (Richard Gilman in *Jubilee*) wrote of Dazai's earlier novel, "Such is the power of art to transfigure what is objectively ignoble or depraved that *The Setting Sun* is actually deeply moving and even inspiriting. . . . To know the nature of despair and to triumph over it in the ways that are possible to oneself—imagination was Dazai's only weapon—is surely a sort of grace."

Donald Keene

PROLOGUE

はしがき

I have seen three pictures of the man.

The first, a childhood photograph you might call it, shows him about the age of ten, a small boy surrounded by a great many women (his sisters and cousins, no doubt). He stands in brightly checked trousers by the edge of a garden pond. His head is tilted at an angle thirty degrees to the left, and his teeth are bared in an ugly smirk. Ugly? You may well question the word, for insensitive people (that is to say, those indifferent to matters of beauty and ugliness) would mechanically comment with a bland,

13

vacuous expression, "What an adorable little boy!"
It is quite true that what commonly passes for
"adorable" is sufficiently present in this child's face
to give a modicum of meaning to the compliment. But
I think that anyone who had ever been subjected to
the least exposure to what makes for beauty would
most likely toss the photograph to one side with the
gesture employed in brushing away a caterpillar, and
mutter in profound revulsion, "What a dreadful
child!"

Indeed, the more carefully you examine the
child's smiling face the more you feel an indescribable,
unspeakable horror creeping over you. You see that
it is actually not a smiling face at all. The boy has
not a suggestion of a smile. Look at his tightly
clenched fists if you want proof. No human being can
smile with his fists doubled like that. It is a monkey.
A grinning monkey-face. The smile is nothing more
than a puckering of ugly wrinkles. The photograph
reproduces an expression so freakish, and at the same
time so unclean and even nauseating, that your impulse is to say, "What a wizened, hideous little boy!"
I have never seen a child with such an unaccountable
expression.

The face in the second snapshot is startlingly unlike the first. He is a student in this picture, although
it is not clear whether it dates from high school or

college days. At any rate, he is now extraordinarily handsome. But here again the face fails inexplicably to give the impression of belonging to a living human being. He wears a student's uniform and a white handkerchief peeps from his breast pocket. He sits in a wicker chair with his legs crossed. Again he is smiling, this time not the wizened monkey's grin but a rather adroit little smile. And yet somehow it is not the smile of a human being: it utterly lacks substance, all of what we might call the "heaviness of blood" or perhaps the "solidity of human life"—it has not even a bird's weight. It is merely a blank sheet of paper, light as a feather, and it is smiling. The picture produces, in short, a sensation of complete artificiality. Pretense, insincerity, fatuousness—none of these words quite covers it. And of course you couldn't dismiss it simply as dandyism. In fact, if you look carefully you will begin to feel that there is something strangely unpleasant about this handsome young man. I have never seen a young man whose good looks were so baffling.

The remaining photograph is the most monstrous of all. It is quite impossible in this one even to guess the age, though the hair seems to be streaked somewhat with grey. It was taken in a corner of an extraordinarily dirty room (you can plainly see in the picture how the wall is crumbling in three places). His small hands are held in front of him. This time he is not smiling. There is no expression whatsoever. The picture has a genuinely chilling, foreboding quality, as if it caught him in the act of dying as he sat before the camera, his hands held over a heater. That is not the only shocking thing about it. The head is shown quite large, and you can examine the features in detail: the forehead is average, the wrinkles on the forehead average, the eyebrows also average, the eyes, the nose, the mouth, the chin . . . the face is not merely devoid of expression, it fails even to leave a memory. It has no individuality. I have only to shut my eyes after looking at it to forget the face. I can remember the wall of the room, the little heater, but all impression of the face of the principal figure in the room is blotted out; I am unable to recall a single thing about it. This face could never be made the subject of a painting, not even of a cartoon. I open my eyes. There is not even the pleasure of recollecting: of course, that's the kind of face it was! To state the matter in the most extreme terms: when I open my eyes and look at the photograph a second time I still cannot remember it. Besides, it rubs against me the wrong way, and makes me feel so uncomfortable that in the end I want to avert my eyes.

I think that even a death mask would hold more of an expression, leave more of a memory. That effigy suggests nothing so much as a human body to which a horse's head has been attached. Something ineffable makes the beholder shudder in distaste. I have never seen such an inscrutable face on a man.

THE FIRST NOTEBOOK

第一の手記

Mine has been a life of much shame.

I can't even guess myself what it must be to live the life of a human being. I was born in a village in the Northeast, and it wasn't until I was quite big that I saw my first train. I climbed up and down the station bridge, quite unaware that its function was to permit people to cross from one track to another. I was convinced that the bridge had been provided to lend an exotic touch and to make the station premises a place of pleasant diversity, like some foreign

21

playground. I remained under this delusion for quite a long time, and it was for me a very refined amusement indeed to climb up and down the bridge. I thought that it was one of the most elegant services provided by the railways. When later I discovered that the bridge was nothing more than a utilitarian device, I lost all interest in it.

Again, when as a child I saw photographs of subway trains in picture books, it never occurred to me that they had been invented out of practical necessity; I could only suppose that riding underground instead of on the surface must be a novel and delightful pastime.

I have been sickly ever since I was a child and have frequently been confined to bed. How often as I lay there I used to think what uninspired decorations sheets and pillow cases make. It wasn't until I was about twenty that I realized that they actually served a practical purpose, and this revelation of human dullness stirred dark depression in me.

Again, I have never known what it means to be hungry. I don't mean by this statement that I was raised in a well-to-do family—I have no such banal intent. I mean that I have had not the remotest idea of the nature of the sensation of "hunger." It sounds peculiar to say it, but I have never been aware that my stomach was empty. When as a boy I returned home from school the people at home would make a great fuss over me. "You must be hungry. We remember what it's like, how terribly hungry you feel by the time you get home from school. How about some jelly beans? There's cake and biscuits too." Seeking to please, as I invariably did, I would mumble that I was hungry, and stuff a dozen jelly beans in my mouth, but what they meant by feeling hungry completely escaped me.

Of course I do eat a great deal all the same, but I have almost no recollection of ever having done so out of hunger. Unusual or extravagant things tempt me, and when I go to the house of somebody else I eat almost everything put before me, even if it takes some effort. As a child the most painful part of the day was unquestionably mealtime, especially in my own home.

At my house in the country the whole family —we were about ten in number—ate together, lined up in two facing rows at table. Being the youngest child I naturally sat at the end. The dining room was dark, and the sight of the ten or more members of the household eating their lunch, or whatever the meal was, in gloomy silence was enough to send chills through me. Besides, this was an old-fashioned country household where the food was more or less prescribed, and it was useless even to hope for unusual or extravagant dishes. I dreaded mealtime more each day. I would sit there at the end of the table in the dimly lit room and, trembling all over as with the cold, I would lift a few morsels of food to my mouth and push them in. "Why must human beings eat three meals every single day? What extraordinarily solemn faces they all make as they eat! It seems to be some kind of ritual. Three times every day at the regulated hour the family gathers in this gloomy room. The places are all laid out in the proper order and, regardless of whether we're hungry or not, we munch our food in silence, with lowered eyes. Who knows? It may be an act of prayer to propitiate whatever spirits may be lurking around the house. . . ." At times I went so far as to think in such terms.

Eat or die, the saying goes, but to my ears it sounded like just one more unpleasant threat. Nevertheless this superstition (I could only think of it as such) always aroused doubt and fear in me. Nothing was so hard for me to understand, so baffling, and at the same time so filled with menacing overtones as the commonplace remark, "Human beings work to earn their bread, for if they don't eat, they die."

In other words, you might say that I still have no understanding of what makes human beings tick. My apprehension on discovering that my concept of happiness seemed to be completely at variance with that of

everyone else was so great as to make me toss sleep-
lessly and groan night after night in my bed. It drove
me indeed to the brink of lunacy. I wonder if I have
actually been happy. People have told me, really more
times than I can remember, ever since I was a small
boy, how lucky I was, but I have always felt as if I
were suffering in hell. It has seemed to me in fact that
those who called me lucky were incomparably more
fortunate than I.

I have sometimes thought that I have been bur-
dened with a pack of ten misfortunes, any one of
which if borne by my neighbor would be enough to
make a murderer of him.

I simply don't understand. I have not the remotest
clue what the nature or extent of my neighbor's woes
can be. Practical troubles, griefs that can be assuaged
if only there is enough to eat—these may be the most
intense of all burning hells, horrible enough to blast
to smithereens my ten misfortunes, but that is precisely
what I don't understand: if my neighbors manage to
survive without killing themselves, without going mad,
maintaining an interest in political parties, not yield-
ing to despair, resolutely pursuing the fight for existence, can their griefs really be genuine? Am I wrong
in thinking that these people have become such complete egoists and are so convinced of the normality
of their way of life that they have never once doubted

themselves? If that is the case, their sufferings should be easy to bear: they are the common lot of human beings and perhaps the best one can hope for. I don't know ... If you've slept soundly at night the morning is exhilarating, I suppose. What kind of dreams do they have? What do they think about when they walk along the street? Money? Hardly—it couldn't only be that. I seem to have heard the theory advanced that human beings live in order to eat, but I've never heard anyone say that they lived in order to make money. No. And yet, in some instances. . . . No, I don't even know that. . . . The more I think of it, the less I understand. All I feel are the assaults of apprehension and terror at the thought that I am the only one who is entirely unlike the rest. It is almost impossible for me to converse with other people. What should I talk about, how should I say it?—I don't know.

This was how I happened to invent my clowning.

It was the last quest for love I was to direct at human beings. Although I had a mortal dread of human beings I seemed quite unable to renounce their society. I managed to maintain on the surface a smile which never deserted my lips; this was the accommodation I offered to others, a most precarious achievement performed by me only at the cost of excruciating efforts within.

As a child I had absolutely no notion of what others, even members of my own family, might be suffering or what they were thinking. I was aware only of my own unspeakable fears and embarrassments. Before anyone realized it, I had become an accomplished clown, a child who never spoke a single truthful word.

I have noticed that in photographs of me taken about that time together with my family, the others all have serious faces; only mine is invariably contorted into a peculiar smile. This was one more variety of my childish, pathetic antics.

Again, I never once answered back anything said to me by my family. The least word of reproof struck me with the force of a thunderbolt and drove me almost out of my head. Answer back! Far from it, I felt convinced that their reprimands were without doubt voices of human truth speaking to me from eternities past; I was obsessed with the idea that since I lacked the strength to act in accordance with this truth, I might already have been disqualified from living among human beings. This belief made me incapable of arguments or self-justification. Whenever anyone criticized me I felt certain that I had been living under the most dreadful misapprehension. I always accepted the attack in silence, though inwardly so terrified as almost to be out of my mind.

It is true, I suppose, that nobody finds it exactly pleasant to be criticized or shouted at, but I see in the face of the human being raging at me a wild animal in its true colors, one more horrible than any lion, crocodile or dragon. People normally seem to be hiding this true nature, but an occasion will arise (as when an ox sedately ensconced in a grassy meadow suddenly lashes out with its tail to kill the horsefly on its flank) when anger makes them reveal in a flash human nature in all its horror. Seeing this happen has always induced in me a fear great enough to make my hair stand on end, and at the thought that this nature might be one of the prerequisites for survival as a human being, I have come close to despairing of myself.

I have always shook with fright before human beings. Unable as I was to feel the least particle of confidence in my ability to speak and act like a human being, I kept my solitary agonies locked in my breast. I kept my melancholy and my agitation hidden, careful lest any trace should be left exposed. I feigned an innocent optimism; I gradually perfected myself in the role of the farcical eccentric.

I thought, "As long as I can make them laugh, it doesn't matter how, I'll be all right. If I succeed in that, the human beings probably won't mind it too much if I remain outside their lives. The one thing

I must avoid is becoming offensive in their eyes: I shall be nothing, the wind, the sky." My activities as jester, a role born of desperation, were extended even to the servants, whom I feared even more than my family because I found them incomprehensible.

In the summer I made everybody laugh by sauntering through the house wearing a red woolen sweater under my cotton kimono. Even my elder brother, who was rarely given to mirth, burst out laughing and commented in intolerably affectionate tones, "That doesn't look so good on you, Yozo." But for all my follies I was not so insensitive to heat and cold as to walk around in a woolen sweater at the height of summer. I had pulled my little sister's leggings over my arms, letting just enough stick out at the opening of the sleeves to give the impression that I was wearing a sweater.

My father frequently had business in Tokyo and maintained a town house for that reason. He spent two or three weeks of the month at a time in the city, always returning laden with a really staggering quantity of presents, not only for members of our immediate family, but even for our relatives. It was a kind of hobby on his part. Once, the night before he was to leave for Tokyo, he summoned all the children to the parlor and smilingly asked us what present we would like this time, carefully noting each child's reply in a little book. It was most unusual for Father to behave so affectionately with the children.

"How about you, Yozo?" he asked, but I could only stammer uncertainly.

Whenever I was asked what I wanted my first impulse was to answer "Nothing." The thought went through my mind that it didn't make any difference, that nothing was going to make me happy. At the same time I was congenitally unable to refuse anything offered to me by another person, no matter how little it might suit my tastes. When I hated something, I could not pronounce the words, "I don't like it." When I liked something I tasted it hesitantly, furtively, as though it were extremely bitter. In either case I was torn by unspeakable fear. In other words, I hadn't the strength even to choose between two alternatives. In this fact, I believe, lay one of the characteristics which in later years was to develop into a major cause of my "life of shame."

I remained silent, fidgeting. My father lost a little of his good humor.

"Will it be a book for you? Or how about a mask for the New Year lion dance? They sell them now in children's sizes. Wouldn't you like one?"

The fatal words "wouldn't you like one?" made it quite impossible for me to answer. I couldn't even think of any suitably clownish response. The jester had completely failed.

"A book would be best, I suppose," my brother said seriously.

"Oh?" The pleasure drained from my father's face. He snapped his notebook shut without writing anything.

What a failure. Now I had angered my father and I could be sure that his revenge would be something fearful. That night as I lay shivering in bed I tried to think if there were still not some way of redressing the situation. I crept out of bed, tiptoed down to the parlor, and opened the drawer of the desk where my father had most likely put his notebook. I found the book and took it out. I riffled through the pages until I came to the place where he had jotted down our requests for presents. I licked the notebook pencil and wrote in big letters LION MASK. This accomplished I returned to my bed. I had not the faintest wish for a lion mask. In fact, I would actually have preferred a book. But it was obvious that Father wanted to buy me a mask, and my frantic desire to cater to his wishes and restore his good humor had emboldened me to sneak into the parlor in the dead of night.

This desperate expedient was rewarded by the great success I had hoped for. When, some days later, my father returned from Tokyo I overheard him say to Mother in his loud voice—I was in the children's room at the time—"What do you think I found when I opened my notebook in the toy shop? See, somebody has written here 'lion mask.' It's not my handwriting. For a minute I couldn't figure it out, then it came to me. This was some of Yozo's mischief. You know, I asked him what he wanted from Tokyo, but he just stood there grinning without saying a word. Later he must have got to wanting that lion mask so badly he couldn't stand it. He's certainly a funny kid. Pretends not to know what he wants and then goes and writes it. If he wanted the mask so much all he had to do was tell me. I burst out laughing in front of everybody in the toy shop. Ask him to come here at once."

On another occasion I assembled all our men and women servants in the foreign-style room. I got one of the menservants to bang at random on the keys of the piano (our house was well equipped with most amenities even though we were in the country), and I made everyone roar with laughter by cavorting in a wild Indian dance to his hit and miss tune. My brother took a flashbulb photograph of me performing my dance. When the picture was developed you could see my peepee through the opening between the two handkerchiefs which served for a loincloth, and this too occasioned much merriment. It was perhaps to be accounted a triumph which surpassed my own expectations.

I used to subscribe regularly to a dozen or more children's magazines and for my private reading ordered books of all sorts from Tokyo. I became an adept in the exploits of Dr. Nonsentius and Dr. Knowitall, and was intimately acquainted with all manner of spooky stories, tales of adventure, collections of jokes, songs and the like. I was never short of material for the absurd stories I solemnly related to make the members of my family laugh.

But what of my schooling?

I was well on the way to winning respect. But the idea of being respected used to intimidate me excessively. My definition of a "respected" man was one who had succeeded almost completely in hoodwinking people, but who was finally seen through by some omniscient, omnipotent person who ruined him and made him suffer a shame worse than death. Even supposing I could deceive most human beings into respecting me, one of them would know the truth, and sooner or later other human beings would learn from him. What would be the wrath and vengeance of those who realized how they had been tricked! That was a hair-raising thought.

I acquired my reputation at school less because I was the son of a rich family than because, in the vulgar parlance, I had "brains." Being a sickly child, I often missed school for a month or two or even a whole school year at a stretch. Nevertheless, when I returned to school, still convalescent and in a rickshaw, and took the examinations at the end of the year, I was always first in my class, thanks to my "brains." I never studied, even when I was well. During recitation time at school I would draw cartoons and in the recess periods I made the other children in the class laugh with the explanations to my drawings. In the composition class I wrote nothing but funny stories. My teacher admonished me, but that didn't make me stop, for I knew that he secretly enjoyed my stories. One day I submitted a story written in a particularly doleful style recounting how when I was taken by my mother on the train to Tokyo, I had made water in a spittoon in the corridor. (But at the time I had not been ignorant that it was a spittoon; I deliberately made my blunder, pretending a childish innocence.) I was so sure that the teacher would laugh that I stealthily followed him to the staff room. As soon as he left the classroom the teacher pulled out my composition from the stack written by my classmates. He began to read as he walked down the hall, and was soon snickering. He went into the staff room and a minute or so later—was it when he finished it?—he burst into loud guffaws, his face scarlet with laughter. I watched him press my paper on the other teachers. I felt very pleased with myself.

A mischievous little imp.

I had succeeded in appearing mischievous. I had succeeded in escaping from being respected. My report card was all A's except for deportment, where it was never better than a C or a D. This too was a source of great amusement to my family.

My true nature, however, was one diametrically opposed to the role of a mischievous imp. Already by that time I had been taught a lamentable thing by the maids and menservants; I was being corrupted. I now think that to perpetrate such a thing on a small child is the ugliest, vilest, cruelest crime a human being can commit. But I endured it. I even felt as if it enabled me to see one more particular aspect of human beings. I smiled in my weakness. If I had formed the habit of telling the truth I might perhaps have been able to confide unabashedly to my father or mother about the crime, but I could not fully understand even my own parents. To appeal for help to any human being —I could expect nothing from that expedient. Supposing I complained to my father or my mother, or to the police, the government—I wondered if in the end I would not be argued into silence by someone in good graces with the world, by the excuses of which the world approved.

It is only too obvious that favoritism inevitably exists: it would have been useless to complain to human beings. So I said nothing of the truth. I felt

I had no choice but to endure whatever came my way and go on playing the clown.

Some perhaps will deride me. "What do you mean by not having faith in human beings? When did you become a Christian anyway?" I fail to see, however, that a distrust for human beings should necessarily lead directly to religion. Is it not true, rather, that human beings, including those who may now be deriding me, are living in mutual distrust, giving not a thought to God or anything else?

There was something that happened when I was a small boy. A celebrated figure of the political party to which my father belonged had come to deliver a speech in our town, and I had been taken by the servants to the theatre to hear him. The house was packed. Everybody in town who was especially friendly to my father was present and enthusiastically applauding. When the speech was over the audience filtered out in threes and fives into the night. As they set out for home on the snow-covered roads they were scathingly commenting on the meeting. I could distinguish among the voices those of my father's closest friends complaining in tones almost of anger about how inept my father's opening remarks had been, and how difficult it was to make head or tail out of the great man's address. Then these men stopped by my house, went into our parlor, and told my father with expressions of genuine delight on their faces what a great success the meeting had been. Even the servants, when asked by my mother about the meeting, answered as if it were their spontaneous thought, that it had been really interesting. These were the self-same servants who had been bitterly complaining on the way home that political meetings are the most boring thing in the world.

This, however, is only a minor example. I am convinced that human life is filled with many pure, happy, serene examples of insincerity, truly splendid of their kind—of people deceiving one another without (strangely enough) any wounds being inflicted, of people who seem unaware even that they are deceiving one another. But I have no special interest in instances of mutual deception. I myself spent the whole day long deceiving human beings with my clowning. I have not been able to work up much concern over the morality prescribed in textbooks of ethics under such names as "righteousness." I find it difficult to understand the kind of human being who lives, or who is sure he can live, purely, happily, serenely while engaged in deceit. Human beings never did teach me that abstruse secret. If I had only known that one thing I should never have had to dread human beings so, nor should I have opposed myself to human life, nor tasted such torments of hell every night. In short, I believe that the reason why I did not tell anyone about that loathesome crime perpetrated on me by the servants was not because of distrust for human beings, nor of course because of Christian leanings, but because the human beings around me had rigorously sealed me off from the world of trust or distrust. Even my parents at times displayed attitudes which were hard for me to understand.

I also have the impression that many women have been able, instinctively, to sniff out this loneliness of mine, which I confided to no one, and this in later years was to become one of the causes of my being taken advantage of in so many ways.

Women found in me a man who could keep a love secret.

THE SECOND NOTEBOOK

第二の手記

On the shore, at a point so close to the ocean one might imagine it was there that the waves broke, stood a row of over twenty fairly tall cherry trees with coal-black trunks. Every April when the new school year was about to begin these trees would display their dazzling blossoms and their moist brown leaves against the blue of the sea. Soon a snowstorm of blossoms would scatter innumerable petals into the water, flecking the surface with points of white which the waves carried back to the shore. This beach

41

strewn with cherry blossoms served as the playground of the high school I attended. Stylized cherry blossoms flowered even on the badge of the regulation school cap and on the buttons of our uniforms.

A distant relative of mine had a house nearby, which was one reason why my father had especially selected for me this school of cherry blossoms by the sea. I was left in the care of the family, whose house was so close to the school that even after the morning bell had rung I could still make it to my class in time if I ran. That was the kind of lazy student I was, but I nevertheless managed, thanks to my accustomed antics, to win popularity with my schoolmates.

This was my first experience living in a strange town. I found it far more agreeable than my native place. One might attribute this, perhaps, to the fact that my clowning had by this time become so much a part of me that it was no longer such a strain to trick others. I wonder, though, if it was not due instead to the incontestable difference in the problem involved in performing before one's own family and strangers, or in one's own town and elsewhere. This problem exists no matter how great a genius one may be. An actor dreads most the audience in his home town; I imagine the greatest actor in the world would be quite paralyzed in a room where all his family and relatives were gathered to watch him. But I had

learned to play my part. I had moreover been quite
a success. It was inconceivable that so talented an
actor would fail away from home.

The fear of human beings continued to writhe
in my breast—I am not sure whether more or less
intensely than before—but my acting talents had unquestionably matured. I could always convulse the
classroom with laughter, and even as the teacher protested what a good class it would be if only I were
not in it, he would be laughing behind his hand. At
a word from me even the military drill instructor,
whose more usual idiom was a barbarous, thunderous
roar, would burst into helpless laughter.

Just when I had begun to relax my guard a bit,
fairly confident that I had succeeded by now in con-
cealing completely my true identity, I was stabbed in
the back, quite unexpectedly. The assailant, like most
people who stab in the back, bordered on being a
simpleton—the puniest boy in the class, whose scrof-
ulous face and floppy jacket with sleeves too long
for him was complemented by a total lack of proficiency in his studies and by such clumsiness in military
drill and physical training that he was perpetually
designated as an "onlooker." Not surprisingly, I failed
to recognize the need to be on my guard against him.

That day Takeichi (that was the boy's name, as
I recall) was as usual "onlooking" during the physical

training period while the rest of us drilled on the horizontal bar. Deliberately assuming as solemn a face as I could muster, I lunged overhead at the bar, shouting with the effort. I missed the bar and sailed on as if I were making a broad jump, landing with a thud in the sand on the seat of my pants. This failure was entirely premeditated, but everybody burst out laughing, exactly as I had planned. I got to my feet with a rueful smile and was brushing the sand from my pants when Takeichi, who had crept up from somewhere behind, poked me in the back. He murmured, "You did it on purpose."

I trembled all over. I might have guessed that someone would detect that I had deliberately missed the bar, but that Takeichi should have been the one came as a bolt from the blue. I felt as if I had seen the world before me burst in an instant into the raging flames of hell. It was all I could do to suppress a wild shriek of terror.

The ensuing days were imprinted with my anxiety and dread. I continued on the surface making everybody laugh with my miserable clowning, but now and then painful sighs escaped my lips. Whatever I did Takeichi would see through it, and I was sure he would soon start spreading the word to everyone he saw. At this thought my forehead broke out in a sweat; I stared around me vacantly with the wild eyes of a madman. If it were possible, I felt, I would like to keep a twenty-four hours a day surveillance over Takeichi, never stirring from him, morning, noon or night, to make sure that he did not divulge the secret. I brooded over what I should do: I would devote the hours spent with him to persuading him that my antics were not "on purpose" but the genuine article; if things went well I would like to become his inseparable friend; but if this proved utterly impossible, I had no choice but to pray for his death. Typically enough, the one thing that never occurred to me was to kill him. During the course of my life I have wished innumerable times that I might meet with a violent death, but I have never once desired to kill anybody. I thought that in killing a dreaded adversary I might actually be bringing him happiness.

In order to win over Takeichi I clothed my face in the gentle beguiling smile of the false Christian. I strolled everywhere with him, my arm lightly around his scrawny shoulders, my head tilted affectionately towards him. I frequently would invite him in honeyed, cajoling tones to come and play in the house where I was lodging. But instead of an answer he always gave me only blank stares in return.

One day after school was let out—it must have been in the early summer—there was a sudden downpour. The other students were making a great fuss about getting back to their lodgings, but since I lived just around the corner, I decided to make a dash for it. Just as I was about to rush outside, I noticed Takeichi hovering dejectedly in the entrance way. I said, "Let's go. I'll lend you my umbrella." I grabbed Takeichi's hand as he hesitated, and ran out with him into the rain. When we arrived home I asked my aunt to dry our jackets. I had succeeded in luring Takeichi to my room.

The household consisted of my aunt, a woman in her fifties, and my two cousins, the older of whom was a tall, frail, bespectacled girl of about thirty (she had been married at one time but was later separated), and the younger a short, round-faced girl who looked fresh out of high school. The ground floor of the house was given over to a shop where small quantities of stationery supplies and sporting goods were offered for sale, but the principal source of income was the rent from the five or six tenements built by my late uncle.

Takeichi, standing haplessly in my room, said, "My ears hurt."

"They must've got wet in the rain." I examined his ears and discovered they were both running horribly. The lobes seemed filled to the bursting with pus. I simulated an exaggerated concern. "This looks terrible. It must hurt." Then, in the gentle tones a woman might use, I apologized, "I'm so sorry I dragged you out in all this rain."

I went downstairs to fetch some cotton wool and alcohol. Takeichi lay on the floor with his head on my lap, and I painstakingly swabbed his ears. Even Takeichi seemed not to be aware of the hypocrisy, the scheming, behind my actions. Far from it—his comment as he lay there with his head pillowed in my lap was, "I'll bet lots of women will fall for you!" —It was his illiterate approximation of a compliment.

This, I was to learn in later years, was a kind of demoniacal prophecy, more horrible than Takeichi could have realized. "To fall for," "to be fallen for" —I feel in these words something unspeakably vulgar, farcical, and at the same time extraordinarily compla-cent. Once these expressions put in an appearance, no matter how solemn the place, the silent cathedrals of melancholy crumble, leaving nothing but an im-pression of fatuousness. It is curious, but the cathe-drals of melancholy are not necessarily demolished if one can replace the vulgar "What a messy business it is to be fallen for" by the more literary "What un-easiness lies in being loved."

Takeichi uttered that idiotic compliment, that women would fall for me, because I had been kind enough to clean the discharge from his ears. My re-action at the time was merely to blush and smile, without saying a word in return but, to tell the truth, I already had a faint inkling of what his prophecy implied. No, to speak in those terms of the atmosphere engendered by so vulgar an expression as "to fall for" is to betray a precocity of sentiment not even worthy of the dialogue of the romantic lead in a musical comedy; I certainly was not moved by the farcical, self-satisfied emotions suggested by the phrase "to have a faint inkling."

I have always found the female of the human species many times more difficult to understand than the male. In my immediate family women outnumbered the men, and many of my cousins were girls. There was also the maidservant of the "crime." I think it would be no exaggeration to say that my only playmates while I was growing up were girls. Nevertheless, it was with very much the sensation of treading on thin ice that I associated with these girls. I could almost never guess their motives. I was in the dark; at times I made indiscreet mistakes which brought me painful wounds. These wounds, unlike the scars from the lashing a man might give, cut inwards very deep, like an internal hemorrhage, bringing intense discomfort. Once inflicted it was extremely hard to recover from such wounds.

Women led me on only to throw me aside; they mocked and tortured me when others were around,

only to embrace me with passion as soon as everyone had left. Women sleep so soundly they seem to
be dead. Who knows? Women may live in order
to sleep. These and various other generalizations
were products of an observation of women since
boyhood days, but my conclusion was that though
women appear to belong to the same species as man,
they are actually quite different creatures, and these
incomprehensible, insidious beings have, fantastic
as it seems, always looked after me. In my case such
an expression as "to be fallen for" or even "to be
loved" is not in the least appropriate; perhaps it
describes the situation more accurately to say that I
was "looked after."

Women were also less demanding than men when
it came to my clowning. When I played the jester men
did not go on laughing indefinitely. I knew that if I
got carried away by my success in entertaining a man
and overdid the role, my comedy would fall flat, and
I was always careful to quit at a suitable place.
Women, on the other hand, have no sense of modera-
tion. No matter how long I went on with my antics
they would ask for more, and I would become exhausted responding to their insatiable demands for
encores. They really laugh an amazing amount of the
time. I suppose one can say that women stuff themselves with far more pleasures than men.

The two cousins in whose house I was living while attending school used to visit my room whenever they had the time. Their knock on my door, no matter how often it came, never failed to startle me so that I almost jumped in fright.

"Are you studying?"

"No," I would say with a smile, shutting my book. I would launch into some silly story, miles removed from what I was thinking. "Today at school the geography teacher, the one we call the Walrus . . ."

One evening my cousins came to my room and after they had compelled me to clown at unmerciful lengths, one of them proposed, "Yozo, let's see how you look with glasses on."

"Why?"

"Don't make such a fuss. Put them on. Here, take these glasses."

They invariably spoke in the same harsh, peremptory tones. The clown meekly put on the older girl's glasses. My cousins were convulsed with laughter.

"You look exactly like him. Exactly like Harold Lloyd."

The American movie comedian was very popular at the time in Japan.

I stood up. "Ladies and gentlemen," I said, raising one arm in greeting, "I should like on this occasion to thank all my Japanese fans—"

I went through the motions of making a speech. They laughed all the harder. From then on whenever a Harold Lloyd movie came to town I went to see it and secretly studied his expressions.

One autumn evening as I was lying in bed reading a book, the older of my cousins—I always called her Sister—suddenly darted into my room quick as a bird, and collapsed over my bed. She whispered through her tears, "Yozo, you'll help me, I know. I know you will. Let's run away from this terrible house together. Oh, help me, please."

She continued in this hysterical vein for a while only to burst into tears again. This was not the first time that a woman had put on such a scene before me, and Sister's excessively emotional words did not surprise me much. I felt instead a certain boredom at their banality and emptiness. I slipped out of bed, went to my desk and picked up a persimmon. I peeled it and offered Sister a section. She ate it, still sobbing, and said, "Have you any interesting books? Lend me something."

I chose Sôseki's *I am a Cat* from my bookshelf and handed it to her.

"Thanks for the persimmon," Sister said as she left the room, an embarrassed smile on her face. Sister was not the only one—I have often felt that I would find it more complicated, troublesome and unpleasant to ascertain the feelings by which a woman lives than to plumb the innermost thoughts of an earthworm. Long personal experience had taught me that when a woman suddenly bursts into hysterics, the way to restore her spirits is to give her something sweet.

Her younger sister, Setchan, would even bring friends to my room, and in my usual fashion I amused them all with perfect impartiality. As soon as a friend had left Setchan would tell me disagreeable things about her, inevitably concluding, "She's a bad girl. You must be careful of her." "If that's the case," I wanted to say, "you needn't have gone to the trouble of bringing her here." Thanks to Setchan almost all the visitors to my room were girls.

This, however, by no means implies that Takeichi's compliment, "Women'll fall for you" had as yet been realized. I was merely the Harold Lloyd of Northeast Japan. Not for some years would Takeichi's silly statement come palpitatingly alive, metamorphosed into a sinister prophecy.

Takeichi made one other important gift to me.

One day he came to my room to play. He was waving a brightly colored picture which he proudly displayed. "It's a picture of a ghost," he explained.

I was startled. That instant, as I could not help feeling in later years, determined my path of escape. I knew what Takeichi was showing me. I knew that it was only the familiar self-portrait of van Gogh. When we were children the French Impressionist School was very popular in Japan, and our first introduction to an appreciation of Western painting most often began with such works. The paintings of van Gogh, Gauguin, Cézanne and Renoir were familiar even to students at country schools, mainly through photographic reproductions. I myself had seen quite a few colored photographs of van Gogh's paintings. His brushwork and the vividness of his colors had intrigued me, but I had never imagined his pictures to be of ghosts.

I took from my bookshelf a volume of Modigliani reproductions, and showed Takeichi the familiar nudes with skin the color of burnished copper. "How about these? Do you suppose they're ghosts too?"

"They're terrific." Takeichi widened his eyes in admiration. "This one looks like a horse out of hell."

"They really are ghosts then, aren't they?"

"I wish I could paint pictures of ghosts like that," said Takeichi.

There are some people whose dread of human beings is so morbid that they reach a point where they yearn to see with their own eyes monsters of ever more horrible shapes. And the more nervous they are —the quicker to take fright—the more violent they pray that every storm will be . . . Painters who have had this mentality, after repeated wounds and intimidations at the hands of the apparitions called human beings, have often come to believe in phantasms—they plainly saw monsters in broad daylight, in the midst of nature. And they did not fob people off with clowning; they did their best to depict these monsters just as they had appeared. Takeichi was right: they had dared to paint pictures of devils. These, I thought, would be my friends in the future. I was so excited I could have wept.

"I'm going to paint too. I'm going to paint pictures of ghosts and devils and horses out of hell." My voice as I spoke these words to Takeichi was lowered to a barely audible whisper, why I don't know.

Ever since elementary school days I enjoyed drawing and looking at pictures. But my pictures failed to win the reputation among my fellow students that my comic stories did. I have never had the least trust in the opinions of human beings, and my stories represented to me nothing more than the clown's gesture of greeting to his audience; they enraptured all of my teachers but for me they were devoid of the slightest interest. Only to my paintings, to the depiction of the object (my cartoons were something else again) did I devote any real efforts of my original though childish style. The copybooks for drawing we used at school were dreary; the teacher's pictures were incredibly inept; and I was obliged to experiment for myself entirely without direction, using every method of expression which came to me. I owned a set of oil paints and brushes from the time I entered high school. I sought to model my techniques on those of the Impressionist School, but my pictures remained flat as paper cutouts, and seemed to offer no promise of ever developing into anything. But Takeichi's words made me aware that my mental attitude towards painting had been completely mistaken. What superficiality—and what stupidity—there is in trying to depict in a pretty manner things which one has thought pretty. The masters through their subjective perceptions created beauty out of trivialities. They did not hide their interest even in things which were nauseatingly ugly, but soaked themselves in the pleasure of depicting them. In other words, they seemed not to rely in the least on the misconceptions of others. Now that I had been initiated by Takeichi into these root secrets of the art of painting, I began to do a few self-portraits, taking care that they not be seen by my female visitors.

The pictures I drew were so heart-rending as to stupefy even myself. Here was the true self I had so desperately hidden. I had smiled cheerfully; I had made others laugh; but this was the harrowing reality. I secretly affirmed this self, was sure that there was no escape from it, but naturally I did not show my pictures to anyone except Takeichi. I disliked the thought that I might suddenly be subjected to their suspicious vigilance, when once the nightmarish reality under the clowning was detected. On the other hand, I was equally afraid that they might not recognize my true self when they saw it, but imagine that it was just some new twist to my clowning—occasion for additional snickers. This would have been most painful of all. I therefore hid the pictures in the back of my cupboard.

In school drawing classes I also kept secret my "ghost-style" techniques and continued to paint as before in the conventional idiom of pretty things.

To Takeichi (and to him alone) I could display my easily wounded sensibilities, and I did not hesitate now to show him my self-portraits. He was very enthusiastic, and I painted two or three more, plus a picture of a ghost, earning from Takeichi the prediction, "You'll be a great painter some day."

Not long afterwards I went up to Tokyo. On my forehead were imprinted the two prophecies uttered by half-wit Takeichi: that I would be "fallen for," and that I would become a great painter.

I wanted to enter an art school, but my father put me into college, intending eventually to make a civil servant out of me. This was the sentence passed

on me and I, who have never been able to answer
back, dumbly obeyed. At my father's suggestion I took
the college entrance examinations a year early and I
passed. By this time I was really quite weary of my
high school by the sea and the cherry blossoms. Once
in Tokyo I immediately began life in a dormitory, but
the squalor and violence appalled me. This time I
was in no mood for clowning; I got the doctor to
certify that my lungs were affected. I left the dormitory and went to live in my father's town house in
Ueno. Communal living had proved quite impossible
for me. It gave me chills just to hear such words as
"the ardor of youth" or "youthful pride": I could
not by any stretch of the imagination soak myself in
"college spirit." The classrooms and the dormitory
seemed like the dumping grounds of distorted sexual
desires, and even my virtually perfected antics were
of no use there.

When the Diet was not in session my father spent
only a week or two of the month at the house. While
he was away there would be just three of us in the
rather imposing mansion—an elderly couple who
looked after the premises and myself. I frequently
cut classes, but not because I felt like sightseeing in
Tokyo. (It looks as if I shall end my days without
ever having seen the Meiji Shrine, the statue of
Kusunoki Masashige or the tombs of the Forty-

Seven *Ronin*.) Instead I would spend whole days in the house reading and painting. When my father was in town I set out for school promptly every morning, although sometimes I actually went to an art class given by a painter in Hongo, and practiced sketching for three or four hours at a time with him. Having been able to escape from the college dormitory I felt rather cynically—this may have been my own bias—that I was now in a rather special position. Even if I attended lectures it was more like an auditor than a regular student. Attending classes became all the more tedious. I had gone through elementary and high schools and was now in college without ever having been able to understand what was meant by school spirit. I never even tried to learn the school songs.

Before long a student at the art class was to initiate me into the mysteries of drink, cigarettes, prostitutes, pawnshops and left-wing thought. A strange combination, but it actually happened that way.

This student's name was Masao Horiki. He had been born in downtown Tokyo, was six years older than myself, and was a graduate of a private art school. Having no atelier at home, he used to attend the art class I frequented, where he was supposedly continuing his study of oil painting.

One day, when we still barely knew each other by sight—we hadn't as yet exchanged a word—he suddenly said to me, "Can you lend me five yen?" I was so taken aback that I ended up by giving him the money.

"That's fine!" he said. "Now for some liquor! You're my guest!"

I couldn't very well refuse, and I was dragged off to a café near the school. This marked the beginning of our friendship.

"I've been noticing you for quite a while. There! That bashful smile—that's the special mark of the promising artist. Now, as a pledge of our friendship —bottoms up!" He called one of the waitresses to our table. "Isn't he a handsome boy? You mustn't fall for him, now. I'm sorry to say it, but ever since he appeared in our art class, I've only been the second handsomest."

Horiki was swarthy, but his features were regular and, most unusual for an art student, he always wore a neat suit and a conservative necktie. His hair was pomaded and parted in the middle.

The surroundings were unfamiliar to me. I kept folding and unfolding my arms nervously, and my smiles now were really bashful. In the course of drinking two or three glasses of beer, however, I began to feel a strange lightness of liberation.

I started, "I've been thinking I'd like to enter a real art school . . ."

"Don't be silly. They're useless. Schools are all useless. The teachers who immerse themselves in Nature! The teachers who show profound sympathy for Nature!"

I felt not the least respect for his opinions. I was thinking, "He's a fool and his paintings are rubbish, but he might be a good person for me to go out with." For the first time in my life I had met a genuine city good-for-nothing. No less than myself, though in a different way, he was entirely removed from the activities of the human beings of the world. We were of one species if only in that we were both disoriented. At the same time there was a basic difference in us: he operated without being conscious of his farcicality or, for that matter, without giving any recognition to the misery of that farcicality.

I despised him as one fit only for amusement, a man with whom I associated for that sole purpose. At times I even felt ashamed of our friendship. But in the end, as the result of going out with him, even Horiki proved too strong for me.

At first, however, I was convinced that Horiki was a nice fellow, an unusually nice fellow, and despite my habitual dread of human beings I relaxed my guard to the extent of thinking that I had found a fine guide to Tokyo. To tell the truth, when I first came to the city, I was afraid to board a streetcar because of the conductor; I was afraid to enter the Kabuki Theatre for fear of the usherettes standing along the sides of the red-carpeted staircase at the main entrance; I was afraid to go into a restaurant because I was intimidated by the waiters furtively hovering behind me waiting for my plate to be emptied. Most of all I dreaded paying a bill—my awkwardness when I handed over the money after buying something did not arise from any stinginess, but from excessive tension, excessive embarrassment, excessive uneasiness and apprehension. My eyes would swim in my head, and the whole world grow dark before me, so that I felt half out of my mind. There was no question of bargaining—not only did I often forget to pick up my change, but I quite frequently forgot to take home the things I had purchased. It was quite impossible for me to make my way around Tokyo by myself. I had no choice but to spend whole days at a time lolling about the house.

So I turned my money over to Horiki and the two of us went out together. He was a great bargainer and—this perhaps earned him the ranking of expert in pleasure-seeking—he displayed unusual proficiency in spending minimal sums of money with maximum effect. His talents extended to getting wherever he wanted in the shortest possible time without ever having recourse to taxis: he used by turns, as seemed appropriate, the streetcar, the bus and even steam launches in the river. He gave me a practical education: thus, if we stopped in the morning at a certain restaurant on our way home from a prostitute's and had a bath with our meal, it was a cheap way of experiencing the sensation of living luxuriously. He also explained that beef with rice or skewered chicken —the sort of dishes you can get at a roadside stand— are cheap but nourishing. He guaranteed that nothing got you drunker quicker than brandy. At any rate, as far as the bill was concerned he never caused me to feel the least anxiety or fear.

Another thing which saved me when with Horiki was that he was completely uninterested in what his listener might be thinking, and could pour forth a continuous stream of nonsensical chatter twenty-four hours a day, in whichever direction the eruption of his "passions" led him. (It may have been that his passions consisted in ignoring the feelings of his listener.) His loquacity ensured that there would be absolutely no danger of our falling into uncomfortable silences when our pleasures had fatigued us. In dealings with other people I had always been on my guard lest those frightful silences occur, but since I was naturally slow of speech, I could only stave them off by a desperate recourse to clowning. Now, however, that stupid Horiki (quite without realizing it) was playing the part of the clown, and I was under no obligation to make appropriate answers. It sufficed if I merely let the stream of his words flow through my ears and, once in a while, commented with a smile, "Not really!"

I soon came to understand that drink, tobacco and prostitutes were all excellent means of dissipating (even for a few moments) my dread of human beings. I came even to feel that if I had to sell every last possession to obtain these means of escape, it would be well worth it.

I never could think of prostitutes as human beings or even as women. They seemed more like imbeciles or lunatics. But in their arms I felt absolute security. I could sleep soundly. It was pathetic how utterly devoid of greed they really were. And perhaps because they felt for me something like an affinity for their kind, these prostitutes always showed me a natural friendliness which never became oppressive. Friendliness with no ulterior motive, friendliness stripped of high-pressure salesmanship, for someone who might never come again. Some nights I saw these imbecile, lunatic prostitutes with the halo of Mary.

I went to them to escape from my dread of human

beings, to seek a mere night of repose, but in the process of diverting myself with these "kindred" prostitutes, I seem to have acquired before I was aware of it a certain offensive atmosphere which clung inseparably to me. This was a quite unexpected by-product of my experience, but gradually it became more manifest, until Horiki pointed it out, to my amazement and consternation. I had, quite objectively speaking, passed through an apprenticeship in women at the hands of prostitutes, and I had of late become quite adept. The severest apprenticeship in women, they say, is with prostitutes, and that makes it the most effective. The odor of the "lady-killer" had come to permeate me, and women (not only prostitutes) instinctively detected it and flocked to me. This obscene and inglorious atmosphere was the "bonus" I received, and it was apparently far more noticeable than the recuperative effects of my apprenticeship.

Horiki informed me of it half as a compliment, I suppose, but it struck a painful chord in me. I remembered now clumsily written letters from bar girls; and the general's daughter, a girl of twenty, whose house was next to mine, and who every morning when I went to school was always hovering around her gate, all dressed up for no apparent reason; and the waitress at the steak restaurant who, even when I didn't say a word . . . ; and the girl at the tobacco shop I patronized who always would put in the package of cigarettes she handed me . . .; and the woman in the seat next to mine at the Kabuki Theatre . . . ; and the time when I was drunk and fell asleep on the streetcar in the middle of the night; and that letter burning with passion that came unexpectedly from a girl relative in the country; and the girl, whoever it was, who left a doll—one she had made herself—for me when I was away. With all of them I had been extremely negative and the stories had gone no further, remaining undeveloped fragments. But it was an undeniable fact, and not just some foolish delusion on my part, that there lingered about me an atmosphere which could send women into sentimental reveries. It caused me a bitterness akin to shame to have this pointed out by someone like Horiki; at the same time I suddenly lost all interest in prostitutes.

To show off his "modernity" (I can't think of any other reason) Horiki also took me one day to a secret Communist meeting. (I don't remember exactly what it was called—a "Reading Society," I think.) A secret Communist meeting may have been for Horiki just one more of the sights of Tokyo. I was introduced to the "comrades" and obliged to buy a pamphlet. I then heard a lecture on Marxian economics delivered by an extraordinarily ugly young man, the guest of honor. Everything he said seemed exceedingly obvious, and undoubtedly true, but I felt sure that something more obscure, more frightening lurked in the hearts of human beings. Greed did not cover it, nor did vanity. Nor was it simply a combination of lust and greed. I wasn't sure what it was, but I felt that there was something inexplicable at the bottom of human society which was not reducible to economics. Terrified as I was by this weird element, I assented to materialism as naturally as water finding its own level. But materialism could not free me from my dread of human beings; I could not feel the joy of hope a man experiences when he opens his eyes on young leaves.

Nevertheless I regularly attended the meetings of the Reading Society. I found it uproariously amusing to see my "comrades," their faces tense as though they were discussing matters of life and death, absorbed in the study of theories so elementary they were on the order of "one and one makes two." I tried to take some of the strain out of the meetings with my usual antics. That was why, I imagine, the oppressive atmosphere of the group gradually relaxed. I came to be so popular that I was considered indispensable at the meetings. These simple people perhaps fancied that I was just as simple as they—an optimistic, laughter-loving comrade—but if such was their view, I was deceiving them completely. I was

not their comrade. Yet I attended every single meeting
and performed for them my full repertory of farce.

I did it because I liked to, because those people
pleased me—and not necessarily because we were
linked by any common affection derived from Marx.

Irrationality. I found the thought faintly pleasur-
able. Or rather, I felt at ease with it. What frightened
me was the logic of the world; in it lay the foretaste of
something incalculably powerful. Its mechanism was
incomprehensible, and I could not possibly remain
closeted in that windowless, bone-chilling room.
Though outside lay the sea of irrationality, it was
far more agreeable to swim in its waters until presently
I drowned.

People talk of "social outcasts." The words apparently denote the miserable losers of the world, the
vicious ones, but I feel as though I have been a "social
outcast" from the moment I was born. If ever I meet
someone society has designated as an outcast, I invariably feel affection for him, an emotion which
carries me away in melting tenderness.

People also talk of a "criminal consciousness." All
my life in this world of human beings I have been
tortured by such a consciousness, but it has been my
faithful companion, like a wife in poverty, and together, just the two of us, we have indulged in our
forlorn pleasures. This, perhaps, has been one of the

attitudes in which I have gone on living. People also commonly speak of the "wound of a guilty conscience." In my case, the wound appeared of itself when I was an infant, and with the passage of time, far from healing it has grown only the deeper, until now it has reached the bone. The agonies I have suffered night after night have made for a hell composed of an infinite diversity of tortures, but—though this is a very strange way to put it—the wound has gradually become dearer to me than my own flesh and blood, and I have thought its pain to be the emotion of the wound as it lived or even its murmur of affection.

For such a person as myself the atmosphere of an underground movement was curiously soothing and agreeable. What appealed to me, in other words, was not so much its basic aims as its personality. The movement served Horiki merely as a pretext for idiotic banter. The only meeting he attended was the one where he introduced me. He gave as his reason for not coming again the stupid joke that Marxists should study not only the productive aspects of society but the consumptive ones. At any rate the consumptive aspects were the only ones we observed together. When I think back on it now, in those days there were Marxists of every variety. Some, like Horiki, called themselves such out of an empty

"modernity." An attraction for its odor of irrationality
led others, like myself, to participate in the movement.

I am sure that if the true believers in Marxism
had discovered what Horiki and I were really interested in, they would have been furious with us,
and driven us out immediately as vile traitors. Strange
to say, however, neither Horiki nor I ever came close
to being expelled. On the contrary, I felt so much
more relaxed in this irrational world than in the world
of rational gentlemen that I was able to do what was
expected of me in a "sound" manner. I was therefore
considered a promising comrade and entrusted with
various jobs fraught with a ludicrous degree of secrecy.
As a matter of fact, I never once refused any of their
jobs. Curiously docile, I performed whatever they
asked of me with such unruffled assurance that the
"dogs" (that was the name by which the comrades
referred to the police) suspected nothing, and I was
never so much as picked up for questioning.

Smiling, making others smile, I punctiliously
acquitted myself of all their "dangerous missions."
(The people in the movement observed such excessive
precautions—they were perpetually prey to life-and-
death tensions—as to suggest some clumsy imitation
of a detective novel. The missions on which I was
employed were really of a stupefying inconsequenti-

ality, but the comrades kept themselves worked up
into a state of frantic excitement by incessantly reminding themselves how dangerous these errands
were.) I felt at the time that if I should become a
party member and got caught, not even the prospect
of spending the rest of my life in prison would bother
me: it occurred to me that prison life might actually
be pleasanter than groaning away my sleepless nights
in a hellish dread of the "realities of life" as led by
human beings.

Even when my father and I were living in the
same house, he was kept so busy receiving guests
or going out that sometimes three or four days elapsed
without our seeing each other. This, however, did
not make his presence any the less oppressive and
intimidating. I was just thinking (without as yet
daring to propose it) how I would like to leave the
house and find lodgings elsewhere, when I learned
from our old caretaker that my father apparently
intended to sell the house.

Father's term of office as a member of the Diet
would soon expire and—doubtless for many reasons—
he seemed to have no intention of standing for election
again. Perhaps (I do not pretend to understand my
father's thoughts any better than those of a stranger)
he had decided to build a retreat somewhere at home.

He never had felt much affection for Tokyo and he must have concluded that it was pointless to maintain a house with servants just for the convenience of a mere college student like myself. At any rate, the house was sold before long and I moved to a gloomy room in an old lodging house in Hongo where I was immediately beset by financial worries.

My father had been giving me a fixed allowance for spending money each month. It would disappear in two or three days' time, but there had always been cigarettes, liquor and fruit in the house, and other things—books, stationery, and anything in the way of clothing—could be charged at shops in the neighborhood. As long as it was one of the shops my father patronized it made no difference even if I left the place without offering so much as a word of explanation.

Then suddenly I was thrown on my own in lodgings, and had to make ends meet on the allowance doled out each month from home. I was quite at my wit's end. The allowance disappeared in the customary two or three days, and I would be almost wild with fright and despair. I sent off barrages of telegrams begging for money of my father, my brothers and my sisters by turns. In the wake of the telegrams went letters giving details. (The facts as stated in the letters were absurd fabrications without exception. I thought it a good strategy to make people laugh when asking favors of them.) Under Horiki's tutelage I also began to frequent the pawnshops. Despite everything I was chronically short of money.

And I was incapable of living all by myself in those lodgings where I didn't know a soul. It terrified me to sit by myself quietly in my room. I felt frightened, as if I might be set upon or struck by someone at any moment. I would rush outside either to help in the activities of the movement or to make the round of the bars with Horiki, drinking cheap saké wherever we went. I almost completely neglected both my school work and my painting. Then in November of my second year in college I got involved in a love suicide with a married woman older than myself. This changed everything.

I had stopped attending classes and no longer devoted a minute of study to my courses; amazingly enough I seemed nevertheless to be able to give sensible answers in the examinations, and I managed somehow to keep my family under the delusion that all was well. But my poor attendance finally caused the school to send my father a confidential report. My elder brother, acting on behalf of my father, thereupon addressed me a long, sternly phrased letter, warning me to change my ways. More pressing causes of grief to me were my lack of money and the jobs required of me by the movement, which had become so frequent and frenetic that I could no longer perform them half in the spirit of fun. I had been chosen leader of all the Marxist student action groups in the schools of central Tokyo. I raced about here and there "maintaining liaison." In my raincoat pocket I carried a little knife I had bought for use in the event of an armed uprising. (I remember now that it had a delicate blade hardly strong enough to sharpen a pencil.) My fondest wish was to drink myself into a sound stupor, but I hadn't the money. Requests for my services came from the party so frequently that I scarcely had time to catch my breath. A sickly body like mine wasn't up to such frantic activity. My only reason all along for helping the group had been my fascination with its irrationality, and to become so horribly involved was a quite unforeseen consequence of my joke. I felt secretly like telling the group, "This isn't my business. Why don't you get a regular party man to do it?" Unable to suppress such reactions of annoyance, I escaped. I escaped, but it gave me no pleasure: I decided to kill myself.

There were at that time three women who showed me special affection. One of them was the landlord's daughter at my lodging house. When I would come back to my room so exhausted by my errands for the movement that I fell into bed without even bothering to eat, she invariably would visit my room, carrying in her hand a writing pad and a pen.

"Excuse me. It's so noisy downstairs with my sister and my little brother that I can't collect my thoughts enough to write a letter." She would seat herself at my desk and write, sometimes for over an hour.

It would have been so much simpler if I just lay there and pretended not to be aware of her, but the girl's looks betrayed only too plainly that she wanted me to talk, and though I had not the least desire to utter a word, I would display my usual spirit of passive service: I would turn over on my belly with a grunt and, puffing on a cigarette, begin, "I'm told that some men heat their bath water by burning the love letters they get from women."

"How horrid! It must be you."

"As a matter of fact, I *have* boiled milk that way —and drunk it too."

"What an honor for the girl! Use mine next time!"

If only she would go, quickly. Letter, indeed! What a transparent pretext that was. I'm sure she was writing the alphabet or the days of the week and the months.

"Show me what you've written," I said, although I wanted desperately to avoid looking at it.

"No, I won't," she protested. "Oh, you're dreadful." Her joy was indecent enough to chill all feeling for her.

I thought up an errand for her to do. "Sorry to bother you, but would you mind going down to the drugstore and buying me some sleeping tablets? I'm over-exhausted. My face is burning so I can't sleep. I'm sorry. And about the money . . ."

"That's all right. Don't worry about the money."

She got up happily. I was well aware that it never offends a woman to be asked to do an errand; they are delighted if some man deigns to ask them a favor.

The second girl interested in me was a "comrade," a student in a teacher's training college. My activities in the movement obliged me, distasteful as it was, to see her every day. Even after the arrangements for the day's job had been completed, she doggedly tagged along after me. She bought me presents, seemingly at random, and offered them with the words, "I wish you would think of me as your real sister."

Wincing at the affectation I would answer, "I do," and force a sad little smile. I was afraid of angering her, and my only thought was to temporize somehow and put her off. As a result, I spent more and more time dancing attendance on that ugly, disagreeable girl. I let her buy me presents (they were without exception in extraordinarily bad taste and I usually disposed of them immediately to the postman or the grocery boy). I tried to look happy when I was with her, and made her laugh with my jokes. One summer evening she simply wouldn't leave me. In the hope of persuading her to go I kissed her when we came to a dark place along the street. She became uncontrollably, shamefully excited. She hailed a taxi and took me to the little room the movement secretly rented in an office building. There we spent the whole night in a wild tumult. "What an extraordinary sister I have," I told myself with a wry smile.

The circumstances were such that I had no way of avoiding the landlord's daughter or this "comrade." Every day we bumped into one another; I could not dodge them as I had various other women in the past. Before I knew what was happening, my chronic lack of assurance had driven me willy-nilly into desperate attempts to ingratiate myself with both of them. It was just as if I were bound to them by some ancient debt.

It was at this same period that I became the unexpected beneficiary of the kindness of a waitress in one of those big cafés on the Ginza. After just one meeting I was so tied by gratitude to her that worry and empty fears paralyzed me. I had learned by this time to simulate sufficiently well the audacity required to board a streetcar by myself or to go to the

Kabuki Theatre or even to a café without any guidance from Horiki. Inwardly I was no less suspicious than before of the assurance and the violence of human beings, but on the surface I had learned bit by bit the art of meeting people with a straight face—no, that's not true: I have never been able to meet anyone without an accompaniment of painful smiles, the buffoonery of defeat. What I had acquired was the technique of stammering somehow, almost in a daze, the necessary small talk. Was this a product of my activities on behalf of the movement? Or of women? Or liquor? Perhaps it was chiefly being hard up for cash that perfected this skill.

I felt afraid no matter where I was. I wondered if the best way to obtain some surcease from this relentless feeling might not be to lose myself in the world of some big café where I would be rubbed against by crowds of drunken guests, waitresses and porters. With this thought in my mind, I went one day alone to a café on the Ginza. I had only ten yen on me. I said with a smile to the hostess who sat beside me, "All I've got is ten yen. Consider yourself warned."

"You needn't worry." She spoke with a trace of a Kansai accent. It was strange how she calmed my agitation with those few words. No, it was not simply because I was relieved of the necessity of worrying about money. I felt, rather, as if being next to her in itself made it unnecessary to worry.

I drank the liquor. She did not intimidate me, and I felt no obligation to perform my clownish antics for her. I drank in silence, not bothering to hide the taciturnity and gloominess which were my true nature.

She put various appetizers on the table in front of me. "Do you like them?" I shook my head. "Only liquor? I'll have a drink too."

It was a cold autumn night. I was waiting at a *sushi* stall back of the Ginza for Tsuneko (that, as I recall, was her name, but the memory is too blurred for me to be sure: I am the sort of person who can forget even the name of the woman with whom he attempted suicide) to get off from work. The *sushi* I was eating had nothing to recommend it. Why, when I have forgotten her name, should I be able to remember so clearly how bad the *sushi* tasted? And I can recall with absolute clarity the close-cropped head of the old man—his face was like a snake's— wagging from side to side as he made the *sushi*, trying to create the illusion that he was a real expert. It has happened to me two or three times since that I have seen on the streetcar what seemed to be a familiar face and wondered who it was, only to realize with a start that the person opposite me looked like the old man from the *sushi* stall. Now, when her name and even her face are fading from my memory, for me to be able to remember that old man's face so accurately I could draw it, is surely a proof of how bad the *sushi* was and how it chilled and distressed me. I should add that even when I have been taken to restaurants famous for *sushi* I have never enjoyed it much.

Tsuneko was living in a room she rented on the second floor of a carpenter's house. I lay on the floor sipping tea, propping my cheek with one hand as if I had a horrible toothache. I took no pains to hide my habitual gloom. Oddly enough, she seemed to like seeing me lie there that way. She gave me the impression of standing completely isolated; an icy storm whipped around her, leaving only dead leaves careening wildly down.

As we lay there together, she told me that she was two years older than I, and that she came from Hiroshima. "I've got a husband, you know. He used to be a barber in Hiroshima, but we ran away to Tokyo together at the end of last year. My husband couldn't find a decent job in Tokyo. The next thing I knew he was picked up for swindling someone, and now he's in jail. I've been going to the prison every day, but beginning tomorrow I'm not going any more."

She rambled on, but I have never been able to get interested when women talk about themselves. It may be because women are so inept at telling a story (that is, because they place the emphasis in the wrong places), or for some other reason. In any case, I have always turned them a deaf ear.

"I feel so unhappy."

I am sure that this one phrase whispered to me would arouse my sympathy more than the longest, most painstaking account of a woman's life. It amazes and astonishes me that I have never once heard a woman make this simple statement. This woman did not say, "I feel so unhappy" in so many words, but something like a silent current of misery an inch wide flowed over the surface of her body. When I lay next to her my body was enveloped in her current, which mingled with my own harsher current of gloom like a "withered leaf settling to rest on the stones at the bottom of a pool." I had freed myself from fear and uneasiness.

It was entirely different from the feeling of being able to sleep soundly which I had experienced in the arms of those idiot-prostitutes (for one thing, the prostitutes were cheerful); the night I spent with that criminal's wife was for me a night of liberation and happiness. (The use of so bold a word, affirmatively, without hesitation, will not, I imagine, recur in these notebooks.)

But it lasted only one night. In the morning, when I woke and got out of bed, I was again the shallow poseur of a clown. The weak fear happiness itself. They can harm themselves on cotton wool. Sometimes they are wounded even by happiness. I was impatient to leave her while things still stood the same, before I got wounded, and I spread my usual smokescreen of farce.

"They say that love flies out the window when poverty comes in the door, but people generally get the sense backwards. It doesn't mean that when a man's money runs out he's shaken off by women. When he runs out of money, he naturally is in the dumps. He's no good for anything. The strength goes out of his laugh, he becomes strangely soured. Finally, in desperation, he shakes off the woman. The proverb means that when a man becomes half-mad, he will shake and shake and shake until he's free of a woman. You'll find that explanation given in the Kanazawa Dictionary, more's the pity. It isn't too hard for me to understand that feeling myself!"

I remember making Tsuneko laugh with just such stupid remarks. I was trying to get away quickly that morning, without so much as washing my face, for I was sure that to stay any longer would be useless and dangerous. Then I came out with that crazy pronouncement on "love flying out the window," which was later to produce unexpected complications.

I didn't meet my benefactor of that night again for a whole month. After leaving her my happiness grew fainter every day that went by. It frightened me even that I had accepted a moment's kindness: I felt I had imposed horrible bonds on myself. Gradually even the mundane fact that Tsuneko had paid the bill at the café began to weigh on me, and I felt as though she was just another threatening woman, like the girl at my lodging house, or the girl from the teacher's training college. Even at the distance which separated us, Tsuneko intimidated me constantly. Besides, I was intolerably afraid that if I met again a woman I had once slept with, I might suddenly burst into a flaming rage. It was my nature to be very timid about meeting people anyway, and so I finally chose the expedient of keeping a safe distance from the Ginza. This timidity of nature was no trickery on my part. Women do not bring to bear so much as a particle of connection between what they do after going to bed and what they do on rising in the morning; they go on living with their world successfully divided in two, as if total oblivion had intervened. My trouble was that I could not yet successfully cope with this extraordinary phenomenon.

At the end of November I went drinking with Horiki at a cheap bar in Kanda. We had no sooner staggered out of that bar than my evil companion

began to insist that we continue our drinking somewhere else. We had already run out of money, but
he kept badgering me.

Finally—and this was because I was drunker and
bolder than usual—I said, "All right. I'll take you
to the land of dreams. Don't be surprised at what you
see. Wine, women and song . . ."

"You mean a café?"

"I do."

"Let's go!" It happened just as simply as that.
The two of us got on a streetcar. Horiki said in high
spirits, "I'm starved for a woman tonight. Is it all
right to kiss the hostess?"

I was not particularly fond of Horiki when he
played the drunk that way. Horiki knew it, and he
deliberately labored the point. "All right? I'm going
to kiss her. I'm going to kiss whichever hostess sits
next to me. All right?"

"It won't make any difference, I suppose."

"Thanks! I'm starved for a woman."

We got off at the Ginza and walked into the café
of "wine, women and song." I was virtually without
a penny, and my only hope was Tsuneko. Horiki and
I sat down at a vacant booth facing each other.
Tsuneko and another hostess immediately hurried
over. The other girl sat next to me, and Tsuneko
plopped herself down beside Horiki. I was taken

aback: Tsuneko was going to be kissed in another few minutes.

It wasn't that I regretted losing her. I have never had the faintest craving for possessions. Once in a while, it is true, I have experienced a vague sense of regret at losing something, but never strongly enough to affirm positively or to contest with others my rights of possession. This was so true of me that some years later I even watched in silence when my own wife was violated.

I have tried insofar as possible to avoid getting involved in the sordid complications of human beings. I have been afraid of being sucked down into their bottomless whirlpool. Tsuneko and I were lovers of just one night. She did not belong to me. It was unlikely that I would pretend to so imperious an emotion as "regret." And yet I was shocked.

It was because I felt sorry for Tsuneko, sorry that she should be obliged to accept Horiki's savage kisses while I watched. Once she had been defiled by Horiki she would no doubt have to leave me. But my ardor was not positive enough for me to stop Tsuneko. I experienced an instant of shock at her unhappiness; I thought, "It's all over now." Then, the next moment, I meekly, helplessly resigned myself. I looked from Horiki to Tsuneko. I grinned.

But the situation took an unexpected turn, one very much for the worse.

"I've had enough," Horiki said with a scowl. "Not even a lecher like myself can kiss a woman who looks so poverty-stricken."

He folded his arms and stared, seemingly in utter disgust, at Tsuneko. He forced a smile.

"Some liquor. I haven't got any money." I spoke under my breath to Tsuneko. I felt I wanted to drink till I drowned in it. Tsuneko was in the eyes of the world unworthy even of a drunkard's kiss, a wretched woman who smelled of poverty. Astonishingly, incredibly enough, this realization struck me with the force of a thunderbolt. I drank more that night than ever before in my life, more . . . more, my eyes swam with drink, and every time Tsuneko and I looked in each other's face, we gave a pathetic little smile. Yes, just as Horiki had said, she really was a tired, poverty-stricken woman and nothing more. But this thought itself was accompanied by a welling-up of a feeling of comradeship for this fellow-sufferer from poverty. (The clash between rich and poor is a hackneyed enough subject, but I am now convinced that it really is one of the eternal themes of drama.) I felt pity for Tsuneko; for the first time in my life I was conscious of a positive (if feeble) movement of love in my heart. I vomited. I passed out. This was also the first time I had ever drunk so much as to lose consciousness.

When I woke Tsuneko was sitting by my pillow. I had been sleeping in her room on the second floor of the carpenter's house. "I thought you were joking when you told me that love flew out the window when poverty came in the door. Were you serious? You didn't come any more. What a complicated business it is, love and poverty. Suppose I work for you? Wouldn't that be all right?"

"No, it wouldn't."

She lay down beside me. Towards dawn she pronounced for the first time the word "death." She too seemed to be weary beyond endurance of the task of being a human being; and when I reflected on my dread of the world and its bothersomeness, on money, the movement, women, my studies, it seemed impossible that I could go on living. I consented easily to her proposal.

Nevertheless I was still unable to persuade myself fully of the reality of this resolution to die. Somehow there lurked an element of make-believe.

The two of us spent that morning wandering around Asakusa. We went into a lunch stand and drank a glass of milk.

She said, "You pay this time."

I stood up, took out my wallet and opened it.

Three copper coins. It was less shame than horror that assaulted me at that moment. I suddenly saw before my eyes my room in the lodging house, absolutely empty save for my school uniform and the bedding—a bleak cell devoid of any object which might be pawned. My only other possessions were the kimono and coat I was wearing. These were the hard facts. I perceived with clarity that I could not go on living.

As I stood there hesitating, she got up and looked inside my wallet. "Is that all you have?"

Her voice was innocent, but it cut me to the quick. It was painful as only the voice of the first woman I had ever loved could be painful. "Is that all?" No, even that suggested more money than I had—three copper coins don't count as money at all. This was a humiliation more strange than any I had tasted before, a humiliation I could not live with. I suppose I had still not managed to extricate myself from the part of the rich man's son. It was then I myself determined, this time as a reality, to kill myself.

We threw ourselves into the sea at Kamakura that night. She untied her sash, saying she had borrowed it from a friend at the café, and left it folded neatly on a rock. I removed my coat and put it in the same spot. We entered the water together.

She died. I was saved.

The incident was treated rather prominently in the press, no doubt because I was a college student. My father's name also had some news value.

I was confined in a hospital on the coast. A relative came from home to see me and take care of necessary arrangements. Before he left he informed me that my father and all the rest of my family were so enraged that I might easily be disowned once and for all. Such matters did not concern me; I thought instead of the dead Tsuneko, and, longing for her, I wept. Of all the people I had ever known, that miserable Tsuneko really was the only one I loved.

A long letter which consisted of a string of fifty stanzas came from the girl at my lodging house. Fifty stanzas, each one beginning with the incredible words, "Please live on for me." The nurses used to visit my sickroom, laughing gaily all the time, and some would squeeze my hand when they left.

They discovered at the hospital that my left lung was affected. This was most fortunate for me: when, not long afterwards, I was taken from the hospital to the police station, charged with having been the accomplice to a suicide, I was treated as a sick man by the police, and quartered not with the criminals but in a special custody room.

Late that night the old policeman standing night duty in the room next to mine softly opened the door.

"Hey," he called to me, "you must be cold. Come here, next to the fire."

I walked into his room, sat on a chair, and warmed myself by the fire. I feigned an air of utter dejection.

"You miss her, don't you?"

"Yes." I answered in a particularly faint and far-away voice.

"That's human nature, I guess." His manner had become increasingly self-important. "Where was it you first took up with this woman?" The question was weighted with an authority almost indistinguishable from that of a judge. My jailor, despising me as a mere child who wouldn't know the difference, acted exactly as if he were charged with the investigation. No doubt he was secretly hoping to while away the long autumn evening by extracting from me a confession in the nature of a pornographic story. I guessed his intent at once, and it was all I could do to restrain the impulse to burst out laughing in his face. I knew that I had the right to refuse to answer any queries put me by the policeman in an "informal interrogation" of this sort, but in order to lend some interest to the long night ahead, I cloaked myself in a kind of simple sincerity, as if I firmly, unquestioningly believed that this policeman was responsible for investigating me, and that the degree of severity of my punishment depended solely on his decision. I made up a confession absurd enough to satisfy— more or less—his prurient curiosity.

"Hmmm. I've got a pretty good idea now. We always take it into consideration when a prisoner answers everything honestly."

"Thank you very much. I hope you will do what you can to help me."

My performance was all but inspired—a great performance which brought me no benefit whatsoever.

In the morning I was called before the police chief. This time it was the real examination.

As soon as I opened the door and entered his office, the police chief said, "There's a handsome lad for you! It wasn't your fault, I can see. Your mother's to blame for having brought such a handsome boy into the world."

He was still young, a dark-complexioned man with something about him which suggested a university education. His words caught me off-guard, and made me as wretched as if I had been born deformed, with a red macula covering half my face.

The examination conducted by this athletic-looking police chief was simple and to the point, a world removed from the furtive, tenaciously obscene "examination" the old policeman had given me the

night before. After he finished his questioning, he
filled out a form to send to the district attorney's
office. He commented as he wrote, "You mustn't
neglect your health that way. You've been coughing
blood, haven't you?"

That morning I had had an odd hawking cough,
and every time I coughed I covered my mouth with
my handkerchief. The handkerchief was spattered
with blood, but it was not blood from my throat. The
night before I had been picking at a pimple under
my ear, and the blood was from that pimple. Realizing at once that it would be to my advantage not to
reveal the truth, I lowered my eyes and sanctimoni-
ously murmured, "Yes."

The police chief finished writing the paper. "It's
up to the district attorney whether or not they bring
action against you, but it would be a good idea to
telephone or telegraph a guarantor to come to the
district attorney's office in Yokohama. There must be
someone, isn't there, who will guarantee you or offer
bail?"

I remembered that a man from my home town,
an antique dealer who was a frequent visitor at my
father's house in Tokyo, had served as my guarantor
at school. He was a short-set man of forty, a bachelor
and a henchman of my father's. His face, particularly
around the eyes, looked so much like a flatfish that my

father always called him by that name. I had also
always thought of him as "Flatfish."

I borrowed the telephone directory at the police
station to look up Flatfish's number. I found it and
called him. I asked if he would mind coming to
Yokohama. Flatfish's tone when he answered was
unrecognizably officious, but he agreed in the end
to be my guarantor.

I went back to the custody room. The police
chief's loud voice reached me as he barked out to
the policeman, "Hey, somebody disinfect the telephone receiver. He's been coughing blood, you know."

In the afternoon they tied me up with a thin
hemp rope. I was allowed to hide the rope under my
coat when we went outside, but the young policeman
gripped the end of the rope firmly. We went to Yokohama on the streetcar.

The experience hadn't upset me in the least. I
missed the custody room in the police station and
even the old policeman. What, I wonder, makes me
that way? When they tied me up as a criminal I
actually felt relieved—a calm, relaxed feeling. Even
now as I write down my recollections of those days
I feel a really expansive, agreeable sensation.

But among my otherwise nostalgic memories
there is one harrowing disaster which I shall never
be able to forget and which even now causes me to
break out into a cold sweat. I was given a brief ex-

amination by the district attorney in his dimly lit office. He was a man of about forty, with an intelligent calm about him which I am tempted to call "honest good looks" (in contrast to my own alleged good looks which, even if true, certainly are tainted with lewdness). He seemed so simple and straightforward that I let down my guard completely. I was listlessly recounting my story when suddenly I was seized with another fit of coughing. I took out my handkerchief. The blood stains caught my eye, and with ignoble opportunism I thought that this cough might also prove useful. I added a couple of extra, exaggerated coughs for good measure and, my mouth still covered by the handkerchief, I glanced at the district attorney's face.

The next instant he asked with his quiet smile, "Was that real?"

Even now the recollection makes me feel so embarrassed I can't sit still. It was worse, I am sure, even than when in high school I was plummeted into hell by that stupid Takeichi tapping me on the back and saying, "You did it on purpose." Those were the two great disasters in a lifetime of acting. Sometimes I have even thought that I should have preferred to be sentenced to ten years imprisonment rather than meet with such gentle contempt from the district attorney.

The charge against me was suspended, but this

brought no joy. I felt utterly wretched as I sat on a bench in the corridor outside the district attorney's office waiting for the arrival of my guarantor, Flatfish.

I could see through the tall windows behind my bench the evening sky glowing in the sunset. Seagulls were flying by in a line which somehow suggested the curve of a woman's body.

THE THIRD NOTEBOOK : PART ONE

第三の手記

一

One of Takeichi's predictions came true, the other went astray. The inglorious prophecy that women would fall for me turned out just as he said, but the happy one, that I should certainly become a great artist, failed to materialize.

I never managed to become anything more impressive than an unknown, second-rate cartoonist employed by the cheapest magazines.

I was expelled from college on account of the

incident at Kamakura, and I went to live in a tiny room on the second floor of Flatfish's house. I gathered that minute sums of money were remitted from home every month for my support, never directly to me, but secretly, to Flatfish. (They apparently were sent by my brothers without my father's knowledge.) That was all—every other connection with home was severed. Flatfish was invariably in a bad humor; even if I smiled to make myself agreeable, he would never return the smile. The change in him was so extraordinary as to inspire me with thoughts of how contemptible—or rather, how comic—human beings are who can metamorphize themselves as simply and effortlessly as they turn over their hands.

Flatfish seemed to be keeping an eye on me, as if I were very likely to commit suicide—he must have thought there was some danger I might throw myself into the sea after the woman—and he sternly forbade me to leave the house. Unable to drink or to smoke, I spent my whole days from the moment I got up until I went to bed trapped in my cubicle of a room, with nothing but old magazines to read. I was leading the life of a half-wit, and I had quite lost even the energy to think of suicide.

Flatfish's house was near the Okubo Medical School. The signboard of his shop, which proclaimed in bold letters "Garden of the Green Dragon, Art and

Antiques," was the only impressive thing about the place. The shop itself was a long, narrow affair, the dusty interior of which contained nothing but shelf after shelf of useless junk. Needless to say, Flatfish did not depend for a living on the sale of this rubbish; he apparently made his money by performing such services as transferring possession of the secret property of one client to another—to avoid taxes. Flatfish almost never waited in the shop. Usually he set out early in the morning in a great hurry, his face set in a scowl, leaving a boy of seventeen to look after the shop in his absence. Whenever this boy had nothing better to do, he used to play catch in the street with the children of the neighborhood. He seemed to consider the parasite living on the second floor a simpleton if not an outright lunatic. He used even to address me lectures in the manner of an older and wiser head. Never having been able to argue with anybody, I submissively listened to his words, a weary though admiring expression on my face. I seemed to recall having heard long ago from the people at home gossip to the effect that this clerk was an illegitimate son of Flatfish, though the two of them never addressed each other as father and son. There must have been some reason for this and for Flatfish's having remained a bachelor, but I am congenitally unable to take much interest in other

people, and I don't know anything beyond what I
have stated. However, there was undoubtedly something strangely fish-like about the boy's eyes, leading
me to wonder if the gossip might not be true. But if
this were the case, this father and son led a re-
markably cheerless existence. Sometimes, late at
night, they would order noodles from a neighborhood
shop—just for the two of them, without inviting me
—and they ate in silence, not exchanging so much
as a word.

The boy almost always prepared the food in
Flatfish's house, and three times a day he would carry
on a separate tray meals for the parasite on the
second floor. Flatfish and the boy ate their meals
in the dank little room under the stairs, so hurriedly
that I could hear the clatter of plates.

One evening towards the end of March Flatfish—
had he enjoyed some unexpected financial success?
or did some other strategem move him? (even supposing both these hypotheses were correct, I imagine
there were a number of other reasons besides of so
obscure a nature that my conjectures could never
fathom them)—invited me downstairs to a dinner
graced by the rare presence of saké. The host himself was impressed by the unwonted delicacy of sliced
tuna, and in his admiring delight he expansively
offered a little saké even to his listless hanger-on.

He asked, "What do you plan to do, in the future I mean?"

I did not answer, but picked up some dried sardines with my chopsticks from a plate on the table and, while I examined the silvery eyes of the little fish, I felt the faint flush of intoxication rise in me. I suddenly became nostalgic for the days when I used to go from bar to bar drinking, and even for Horiki. I yearned with such desperation for "freedom" that I became weak and tearful.

Ever since coming to this house I had lacked all incentive even to play the clown; I had merely lain prostrate under the contemptuous glances of Flatfish and the boy. Flatfish himself seemed disinclined to indulge in long, heart-to-heart talks, and for my part no desire stirred within me to run after him with complaints.

Flatfish pursued his discourse. "As things stand it appears that the suspended sentence passed against you will not count as a criminal record or anything of that sort. So, you see, your rehabilitation depends entirely on yourself. If you mend your ways and bring me your problems—seriously, I mean—I will certainly see what I can do to help you."

Flatfish's manner of speech—no, not only his, but the manner of speech of everybody in the world —held strange, elusive complexities, intricately presented with overtones of vagueness: I have always been baffled by these precautions so strict as to be useless, and by the intensely irritating little maneuvers surrounding them. In the end I have felt past caring; I have laughed them away with my clowning, or surrendered to them abjectly with a silent nod of the head, in the attitude of defeat.

In later years I came to realize that if Flatfish had at the time presented me with a simple statement of the facts, there would have been no untoward consequences. But as a result of his unnecessary precautions, or rather, of the incomprehensible vanity and love of appearances of the people of the world, I was subjected to a most dismal set of experiences.

How much better things would have been if only Flatfish had said something like this, "I'd like you to enter a school beginning in the April term. Your family has decided to send you a more adequate allowance once you have entered school."

Only later did I learn that this in fact was the situation. If I had been told that, I should probably have done what Flatfish asked. But thanks to his intolerably prudent, circumlocutious manner of speech, I only felt irritable, and this caused the whole course of my life to be altered.

"If you do not feel like confiding your problems to me I'm afraid there's nothing I can do for you."

"What kind of problems?" I really had no idea what he was driving at.

"Isn't there something weighing on your heart?"

"For example?"

" 'For example'! What do you yourself want to do now?"

"Do you think I ought to get a job?"

"No, don't ask me. Tell me what you would really like."

"But even supposing I said I wanted to go back to school . . ."

"Yes, I know, it costs money. But the question is not the money. It's what you feel."

Why, I wonder, couldn't he have mentioned the simple fact that the money would be forthcoming from home? That one fact would probably have settled my feelings, but I was left in a fog.

"How about it? Have you anything which might be described as aspirations for the future? I suppose one can't expect people one helps to understand how difficult it is to help another person."

"I'm sorry."

"I'm really worried about you. I'm responsible for you now, and I don't like you to have such half-hearted feelings. I wish you would show me that you're resolved to make a real effort to turn over a new leaf. If, for example, you were to come to me to discuss seriously your plans for the future, I would certainly do what I could. But of course you can't expect to lead your former life of luxury on the help that poor old Flatfish can give—don't give yourself any illusions on that score. No—but if you are resolute in your determination to begin again afresh, and you make definite plans for building your future, I think I might actually be willing to help you to rehabilitate yourself if you came to me for help, though Heaven knows I haven't much to spare. Do you understand my feelings? What *are* your plans?"

"If you won't let me stay here in your house I'll work . . ."

"Are you serious? Do you realize that nowadays even graduates of Tokyo Imperial University . . ."

"No, I wasn't thinking of getting a job with a company."

"What then?"

"I want to be a painter." I said this with conviction.

"Wha-a-t?"

I can never forget the indescribably crafty shadow that passed over Flatfish's face as he laughed at me, his neck drawn in. It resembled contempt, yet it was different: if the world, like the sea, had depths of a thousand fathoms, this was the kind of weird shadow which might be found hovering here and there at the bottom. It was a laugh which enabled me to catch a glimpse of the very nadir of adult life.

He said, "There's no point in discussing such a thing. Your feelings are still all up in the air. Think it over. Please devote this evening to thinking it over seriously."

I ran up to the second floor as though driven, but even when I lay in bed nothing of a particularly constructive nature occurred to me. The next morning at dawn I ran away from Flatfish's house.

I left behind a note, scrawled in pencil in big letters on my writing pad. "I shall return tonight without fail. I am going to discuss my plans for the future with a friend who lives at the address below. Please don't worry about me. I'm telling the truth." I wrote Horiki's name and address, and stole out of Flatfish's house.

I did not run away because I was mortified at having been lectured by Flatfish. I was, exactly as Flatfish described, a man whose feelings were up in the air, and I had absolutely no idea about future plans or anything else. Besides, I felt rather sorry for Flatfish that I should be a burden on him, and I found it quite intolerably painful to think that if by some remote chance I felt like bestirring myself to achieve a worthy purpose, I should have to depend on poor old Flatfish to dole out each month the capital needed for my rehabilitation.

When I left Flatfish's house, however, I was certainly not seriously entertaining any idea of consulting the likes of Horiki about my future plans. I left the note hoping thereby to pacify Flatfish for a little while, if only for a split-second. (I didn't write the note so much out of a detective-story strategem to gain a little more time for my escape—though, I must admit that the desire was at least faintly present —as to avoid causing Flatfish a sudden shock which would send him into a state of wild alarm and confusion. I think that might be a somewhat more accurate presentation of my motives. I knew that the facts were certain to be discovered, but I was afraid to state them as they were. One of my tragic flaws is the compulsion to add some sort of embellishment to every situation—a quality which has made people call me at times a liar—but I have almost never embellished in order to bring myself any advantage; it was rather that I had a strangulating fear of that cataclysmic change in the atmosphere the instant the flow of a conversation flagged, and even when I knew that it would later turn to my disadvantage, I frequently felt obliged to add, almost inadvertently, my word of embellishment, out of a desire to please born of my usual desperate mania for service. This may have been a twisted form of my weakness, an idiocy, but the habit it engendered was taken full advantage of by the so-called honest citizens of the world.) That was how I happened to jot down Horiki's name and address as they floated up from the distant recesses of my memory.

After leaving Flatfish's house I walked as far as Shinjuku, where I sold the books I had in my pockets. Then I stood there uncertainly, utterly at a loss what to do. Though I have always made it my practice to be pleasant to everybody, I have not once actually experienced friendship. I have only the most painful recollections of my various acquaintances with the exception of such companions in pleasure as Horiki. I have frantically played the clown in order to disentangle myself from these painful relationships, only to wear myself out as a result. Even now it comes as a shock if by chance I notice in the street a face resembling someone I know however slightly, and I am at once seized by a shivering violent enough to make me dizzy. I know that I am liked by other people, but I seem to be deficient in the faculty to love others. (I should add that I have very strong doubts as to whether even human beings really possess this faculty.) It was hardly to be expected that someone like myself could ever develop any close friendships—besides, I lacked even the ability to pay visits. The front door of another person's house terrified me more than the gate of Inferno in the *Divine Comedy*, and I am not exaggerating when I say that I really felt I could detect within the door the presence of a horrible dragon-like monster writhing there with a dank, raw smell.

I had no friends. I had nowhere to go.

Horiki.

Here was a real case of a true word having been said in jest: I decided to visit Horiki, exactly as I had stated in my farewell note to Flatfish. I had never before gone myself to Horiki's house. Usually I would invite him to my place by telegram when I wanted to see him. Now, however, I doubted whether I could manage the telegraph fee. I also wondered, with the jaundiced intelligence of a man in disgrace, whether Horiki might not refuse to come even if I telegraphed him. I decided on a visit, the most difficult thing in the world for me. Giving vent to a sigh, I boarded the streetcar. The thought that the only hope left me in the world was Horiki filled me with a foreboding dreadful enough to send chills up and down my spine.

Horiki was at home. He lived in a two-storied house at the end of a dirty alley. Horiki occupied only one medium-sized room on the second floor; downstairs his parents and a young workman were busily stitching and pounding strips of cloth to make thongs for sandals.

Horiki showed me that day a new aspect of his city-dweller personality. This was his knowing nature, an egoism so icy, so crafty that a country boy like myself could only stare with eyes opened wide in amazement. He was not a simple, endlessly passive type like myself.

"You. What a surprise. You've been forgiven by your father, have you? Not yet?"

I was unable to confess that I had run away.

In my usual way I evaded the issue, though I was certain that Horiki soon, if not immediately, would grasp what had happened. "Things will take care of themselves, in one way or another."

"Look here! It's no laughing matter. Let me give you a word of advice—stop your foolishness here and now. I've got business today anyway. I'm awfully busy these days."

"Business? What kind of business?"

"Hey! What are you doing there? Don't tear the thread off the cushion!"

While we were talking I had unconsciously been fiddling with and twisting around my finger one of the tassel-like threads which protruded from the corners of the cushion on which I sat—binding-threads, I think they are called. Horiki had assumed a jealous possessiveness about everything in his house down to the last cushion thread, and he glared at me, seemingly quite unembarrassed by this attitude. When I think of it, Horiki's acquaintanceship with me had cost him nothing.

Horiki's aged mother brought in a tray with two dishes of jelly.

"What have we here?" Horiki asked his mother tenderly, in the tones of the truly dutiful son, continuing in language so polite it sounded quite unnatural. "Oh, I'm sorry. Have you made jelly? That's terrific. You shouldn't have bothered. I was just going out on some business. But it would be wicked not to eat your wonderful jelly after you've gone to all the trouble. Thank you so much." Then, turning in my direction, "How about one for you? Mother made it specially. Ahh . . . this is delicious. Really terrific."

He ate with a gusto, almost a rapture, which did not seem to be altogether play acting. I also spooned my bowl of jelly. It tasted watery, and when I came to the piece of fruit at the bottom, it was not fruit after all, but a substance I could not identify. I by no means despised their poverty. (At the time I didn't think that the jelly tasted bad, and I was really grateful for the old woman's kindness. It is true that I dread poverty, but I do not believe I ever have despised it.) The jelly and the way Horiki rejoiced

over it taught me a lesson in the parsimoniousness
of the city-dweller, and in what it is really like in a
Tokyo household where the members divide their
lives so sharply between what they do at home and
what they do on the outside. I was filled with dismay
at these signs that I, a fool rendered incapable by
my perpetual flight from human society from dis-
tinguishing between "at home" and "on the outside,"
was the only one completely left out, that I had been
deserted even by Horiki. I should like to record that
as I manipulated the peeling lacquer chopsticks to
eat my jelly, I felt unbearably lonely.

"I'm sorry, but I've got an appointment today,"
Horiki said, standing and putting on his jacket. "I'm
going now. Sorry."

At that moment a woman visitor arrived for
Horiki. My fortunes thereby took a sudden turn.

Horiki at once became quite animated. "Oh, I
am sorry. I was just on my way to your place when this
fellow dropped in without warning. No, you're not
in the way at all. Please come in."

He seemed rattled. I took the cushion from under
me and turned it over before handing it to Horiki,
but snatching it from my hands, he turned it over
once more as he offered it to the woman. There was
only that one cushion for guests, besides the cushion
Horiki sat on.

The woman was a tall, thin person. She declined the cushion and sat demurely in a corner by the door.

I listened absent-mindedly to their conversation. The woman, evidently an employee of a magazine publisher, had commissioned an illustration from Horiki, and had come now to collect it.

"We're in a terrible hurry," she explained.

"It's ready. It's been ready for some time. Here you are."

A messenger arrived with a telegram.

As Horiki read it I could see the good spirits on his face turn ugly. "Damn it, what have you been up to?"

The telegram was from Flatfish.

"You go back at once. I ought to take you there myself, I suppose, but I haven't got the time now. Imagine—a runaway, and looking so smug!"

The woman asked, "Where do you live?"

"In Okubo," I answered without thinking.

"That's quite near my office."

She was born in Koshu and was twenty-eight. She lived in an apartment in Koenji with her five-year-old girl. She told me that her husband had died three years before.

"You look like someone who's had an unhappy childhood. You're so sensitive—more's the pity for you."

I led for the first time the life of a kept man. After Shizuko (that was the name of the lady journalist) went out to work in the morning at the magazine publisher's, her daughter Shigeko and I obediently looked after the apartment. Shigeko had always been left to play in the superintendent's room while her mother was away, and now she seemed delighted that an interesting "uncle" had turned up as a new playmate.

For about a week I remained in a state of daze. Just outside the apartment window was a kite caught in the telegraph wires; blown about and ripped by the dusty spring wind, it nevertheless clung tenaciously to the wires, as if in affirmation of something. Every time I looked at the kite I had to smile with embarrassment and blush. It haunted me even in dreams.

"I want some money."

"How much?" she asked.

"A lot . . . Love flies out the window when poverty comes in the door, they say, and it's true."

"Don't be silly. Such a trite expression."

"Is it? But you don't understand. I may run away if things go on at this rate."

"Which of us is the poor one? And which will run away? What a silly thing to say!"

"I want to buy my drinks and cigarettes with my own money. I'm a lot better artist than Horiki."

At such times the self-portraits I painted in high

school—the ones Takeichi called "ghost pictures" —naturally came to mind. My lost masterpieces. These, my only really worthwhile pictures, had disappeared during one of my frequent changes of address. I afterwards painted pictures of every description, but they all fell far, far short of those splendid works as I remembered them. I was plagued by a heavy sense of loss, as if my heart had become empty.

The undrunk glass of absinthe.

A sense of loss which was doomed to remain eternally unmitigated stealthily began to take shape. Whenever I spoke of painting, that undrunk glass of absinthe flickered before my eyes. I was agonized by the frustrating thought: if only I could show them those paintings they would believe in my artistic talents.

"Do you really? You're adorable when you joke that way with a serious face."

But it was no joke. It was true. I wished I could have shown her those pictures. I felt an empty chagrin which suddenly gave way to resignation. I added, "Cartoons, I mean. I'm sure I'm better than Horiki at cartoons if nothing else."

These clownish words of deceit were taken more seriously than the truth.

"Yes, that's so. I've really been struck by those

cartoons you're always drawing for Shigeko. I've
burst out laughing over them myself. How would you
like to draw for our magazine? I can easily ask the
editor."

Her company published a monthly magazine, not
an especially notable one, for children.

"Most women have only to lay eyes on you to
want to be doing something for you so badly they
can't stand it . . . You're always so timid and yet
you're funny . . . Sometimes you get terribly lone-
some and depressed, but that only makes a woman's
heart itch all the more for you."

Shizuko flattered me with these and other com-
ments which, with the special repulsive quality of
the kept man, I calmly accepted. Whenever I thought
of my situation I sank all the deeper in my depression,
and I lost all my energy. It kept preying on my mind
that I needed money more than a woman, that anyway I wanted to escape from Shizuko and make my
own living. I made plans of every sort, but my struggles only enmeshed me the more in my dependence
on her. This strong-minded woman herself dealt with
the complications which developed from my running
away, and took care of almost everything else for me.
As a result I became more timid than ever before
her.

At Shizuko's suggestion a conference took place

attended by Flatfish, Horiki and herself at which it was concluded that all relations between me and my family were to be broken, and I was to live with Shizuko as man and wife. Thanks also to Shizuko's efforts, my cartoons began to produce a surprising amount of money. I bought liquor and cigarettes, as I had planned, with the proceeds, but my gloom and depression grew only the more intense. I had sunk to the bottom: sometimes when I was drawing "The Adventures of Kinta and Ota," the monthly comic strip for Shizuko's magazine, I would suddenly think of home, and this made me feel so miserable that my pen would stop moving, and I looked down, through brimming tears.

At such times the one slight relief came from little Shigeko. By now she was calling me "Daddy" with no show of hesitation.

"Daddy, is it true that God will grant you anything if you pray for it?"

I thought that I for one would like to make such a prayer:

Oh, vouchsafe unto me a will of ice. Acquaint me with the true natures of "human beings." Is it not a sin for a man to push aside his fellow? Vouchsafe unto me a mask of anger.

"Yes. I'm sure He'll grant Shigeko anything she wants, but I don't suppose Daddy has a chance."

I was frightened even by God. I could not believe in His love, only in His punishment. Faith. That, I felt, was the act of facing the tribunal of justice with one's head bowed to receive the scourge of God. I could believe in hell, but it was impossible for me to believe in the existence of heaven.

"Why haven't you a chance?"

"Because I disobeyed what my father told me."

"Did you? But everybody says you're so nice."

That's because I deceived them. I was aware that everybody in the apartment house was friendly to me, but it was extremely difficult for me to explain to Shigeko how much I feared them all, and how I was cursed by the unhappy peculiarity that the more I feared people the more I was liked, and the more I was liked the more I feared them—a process which eventually compelled me to run away from everybody.

I casually changed the subject. "Shigeko, what would you like from God?"

"I would like my real Daddy back."

I felt dizzy with the shock. An enemy. Was I Shigeko's enemy, or was she mine? Here was another frightening grown-up who would intimidate me. A stranger, an incomprehensible stranger, a stranger full of secrets. Shigeko's face suddenly began to look that way.

I had been deluding myself with the belief that

Shigeko at least was safe, but she too was like the ox which suddenly lashes out with its tail to kill the horsefly on its flank. I knew that from then on I would have to be timid even before that little girl.

"Is the lady-killer at home?"

Horiki had taken to visiting me again at my place. I could not refuse him, even though this was the man who had made me so miserable the day I ran away. I welcomed him with a feeble smile.

"Your comic strips are getting quite a reputation, aren't they? There's no competing with amateurs—they're so foolhardy they don't know when to be afraid. But don't get overconfident. Your composition is still not worth a damn."

He dared to act the part of the master to me! I felt my usual empty tremor of anguish at the thought, "I can imagine the expression on his face if I showed him my 'ghost pictures'." But I protested instead, "Don't say such things. You'll make me cry."

Horiki looked all the more elated with himself. "If all you've got is just enough talent to get along, sooner or later you'll betray yourself."

Just enough talent to get along—I really had to smile at that. Imagine saying that I had enough talent to get along! It occurred to me that a man like myself who dreads human beings, shuns and deceives them, might on the surface seem strikingly like another man who reveres the clever, wordly-wise rules for success embodied in the proverb "Let sleeping dogs lie." Is it not true that no two human beings under-stand anything whatsoever about each other, that those who consider themselves bosom friends may be utterly mistaken about their fellow and, failing to realize this sad truth throughout a lifetime, weep when they read in the newspapers about his death?

Horiki, I had to admit, participated in the settle-ment after my running away, though reluctantly, under pressure from Shizuko, and he was now be-having exactly like the great benefactor to whom I owed my rehabilitation or like the go-between of a romance. The look on his face as he lectured me was grave. Sometimes he would barge in late at night, dead-drunk, to sleep at my place, or stop by to borrow five yen (invariably five yen).

"You must stop your fooling around with women. You've gone far enough. Society won't stand for more."

What, I wondered, did he mean by "society"? The plural of human beings? Where was the sub-stance of this thing called "society"? I had spent my whole life thinking that society must certainly be something powerful, harsh and severe, but to hear Horiki talk made the words "Don't you mean yourself?" come to the tip of my tongue. But I held the words back, reluctant to anger him.

Society won't stand for it.

It's not society. You're the one who won't stand for it—right?

If you do such a thing society will make you suffer for it.

It's not society. It's you, isn't it?

Before you know it, you'll be ostracized by society.

It's not society. You're going to do the ostracizing, aren't you?

Words, words of every kind went flitting through my head. "Know thy particular fearsomeness, thy knavery, cunning and witchcraft!" What I said, however, as I wiped the perspiration from my face with a handkerchief was merely, "You've put me in a cold sweat!" I smiled.

From then on, however, I came to hold, almost as a philosophical conviction, the belief: What is society but an individual?

From the moment I suspected that society might be an individual I was able to act more in accordance with my own inclinations. Shizuko found that I had become rather self-willed and not so timid as before. Horiki remarked that it was funny how stingy I had become. Or, as Shigeko had it, I had stopped being so nice to Shigeko.

Without a word, without a trace of a smile, I spent one day after the next looking after Shigeko and drawing comic strips, some of them so idiotic I couldn't understand them myself, for the various firms which commissioned them. (Orders had gradually started coming in from other publishers, all of an even lower class than Shizuko's company—third-rate publishers, I suppose they'd be called.) I drew with extremely, excessively depressed emotions, deliberately penning each line, only to earn money for drink. When Shizuko came home from work I would dash out as if in relay with her, and head for the outdoor booths near the station to drink cheap, strong liquor.

Somewhat buoyed after a bout, I would return to the apartment. I would say, "The more I look at you the funnier your face seems. Do you know I get inspiration for my cartoons from looking at your face when you're asleep?"

"What about your face when you sleep? You look like an old man, a man of forty."

"It's all your fault. You've drained me dry. 'Man's life is like a flowing river. What is there to fret over? On the river bank a willow tree . . .'"

"Hurry to bed and stop making such a racket.

Would you like something to eat?" She was quite calm. She did not take me seriously.

"If there's any liquor left, I'll drink it. 'Man's life is like a flowing river. Man's river . . .' no, I mean 'the river flows, the flowing life'."

I would go on singing as Shizuko took off my clothes. I fell asleep with my forehead pressed against her breast. This was my daily routine.

. . . et puis on recommence encore le lendemain
avec seulement la même règle que la veille
et qui est d'éviter les grandes joies barbares
de même que les grandes douleurs
comme un crapaud contorne une pierre sur son
    chemin. . . .

When I first read in translation these verses by Guy-Charles Cros, I blushed until my face burned.

The toad.

(That is what I was—a toad. It was not a question of whether or not society tolerated me, whether or not it ostracized me. I was an animal lower than a dog, lower than a cat. A toad. I sluggishly moved—that's all.)

The quantities of liquor I consumed had gradually increased. I went drinking not only in the neighborhood of the Koenji station but as far as the Ginza.

Sometimes I spent the night out. At bars I acted the part of a ruffian, kissed women indiscriminately, did anything as long as it was not in accord with "accepted usage," drank as wildly—no more so—as before my attempted suicide, was so hard pressed for money that I used to pawn Shizuko's clothes.

A year had passed since I first came to her apartment and smiled bitterly at the torn kite. One day, along when the cherry trees were going to leaf, I stole some of Shizuko's underrobes and sashes, and took them to a pawnshop. I used the money they gave me to go drinking on the Ginza. I spent two nights in a row away from home. By the evening of the third day I began to feel some compunctions about my behavior, and I returned to Shizuko's apartment. I unconsciously hushed my footsteps as I approached the door, and I could hear Shizuko talking with Shigeko.

"Why does he drink?"

"It's not because he likes liquor. It's because he's too good, because . . ."

"Do all good people drink?"

"Not necessarily, but . . ."

"I'm sure Daddy'll be surprised."

"Maybe he won't like it. Look! It's jumped out of the box."

"Like the funny man in the comics he draws."

"Yes, isn't it?" Shizuko's low laugh sounded genuinely happy.

I opened the door a crack and looked in. I saw a small white rabbit bounding around the room. The two of them were chasing it.

(They were happy, the two of them. I'd been a fool to come between them. I might destroy them both if I were not careful. A humble happiness. A good mother and child. God, I thought, if you listen to the prayers of people like myself, grant me happiness once, only once in my whole lifetime will be enough! Hear my prayer!)

I felt like getting down on my knees to pray then and there. I shut the door softly, went to the Ginza, and did not return to the apartment.

My next spell as a kept man was in an apartment over a bar close by the Kyobashi Station.

Society. I felt as though even I were beginning at last to acquire some vague notion of what it meant. It is the struggle between one individual and another, a then-and-there struggle, in which the immediate triumph is everything. *Human beings never submit to human beings.* Even slaves practice their mean retaliations. Human beings cannot conceive of any means of survival except in terms of a single then-and-there contest. They speak of duty to one's country and suchlike things, but the object of their efforts is invariably the individual, and, even once the individual's needs have been met, again the individual comes in. The incomprehensibility of society is the incomprehensibility of the individual. The ocean is not society; it is individuals. This was how I managed to gain a modicum of freedom from my terror at the illusion of the ocean called the world. I learned to behave rather aggressively, without the endless anxious worrying I knew before, responding as it were to the needs of the moment.

When I left the apartment in Koenji I told the madam of the bar in Kyobashi, "I've left her and come to you." That was all I said, and it was enough. In other words, my single then-and-there contest had been decided, and from that night I lodged myself without ceremony on the second floor of her place. "Society" which by all rights should have been implacable, inflicted not a particle of harm on me, and I offered no explanations. As long as the madam was so inclined, everything was all right.

At the bar I was treated like a customer, like the owner, like an errand boy, like a relative of the management; one might have expected that I would be considered a very dubious character, but "society" was not in the least suspicious of me, and the regular customers of the bar treated me with almost painful kindness. They called me by my first name and bought me drinks.

I gradually came to relax my vigilance towards the world. I came to think that it was not such a dreadful place. My feelings of panic had been molded by the unholy fear aroused in me by such superstitions of science as the hundreds of thousands of whooping-cough germs borne by the spring breezes, the hundreds of thousands of eye-destroying bacteria which infest the public baths, the hundreds of thousands of microbes in a barber shop which will cause baldness, the swarms of scabious parasites infecting the leather straps in the subway cars; or the tapeworm, fluke and heaven knows what eggs that undoubtedly lurk in raw fish and in undercooked beef and pork; or the fact that if you walk barefoot a tiny sliver of glass may penetrate the sole of your foot and after circulating through your body reach the eye and cause blindness. There is no disputing the accurate, scientific fact that millions of germs are floating, swimming, wriggling everywhere. At the same time, however, if you ignore them completely they lose all possible connection with yourself, and at once become nothing more than vanishing "ghosts of science." This too I came to understand. I had been so terrorized by scientific statistics (if ten million people each leave over three grains of rice from their lunch, how many sacks of rice are wasted in one day; if ten million people each economize one paper handkerchief a day, how much pulp will be saved?) that whenever I left over a single grain of rice, whenever I blew my nose, I imagined that I was wasting mountains of rice, tons of paper, and I fell prey to a mood dark as if I had committed some terrible crime. But these were the lies of science, the lies of statistics and mathematics: you can't collect three grains of rice from everybody. Even as an exercise in multiplication or division, it ranks as one of the most elementary and feeble-minded problems, about on a par with the computation of the percentage of times that people slip in dark, unlighted bathrooms and fall into the toilet, or the percentage of passengers who get their feet caught in the space between the door of a subway train and the edge of the platform, or other such footling exercises in probability. These events seem entirely within the bounds of possibility, but I have never heard a single instance of anyone hurting himself by falling into the toilet. I felt pity and contempt for the self which until yesterday had accepted such hypothetical situations as eminently factual scientific truths and was terrified by them. This shows the degree to which I had bit by bit arrived at a knowledge of the real nature of what is called the world.

Having said that, I must now admit that I was

still afraid of human beings, and before I could meet even the customers in the bar I had to fortify myself by gulping down a glass of liquor. The desire to see frightening things—that was what drew me every night to the bar where, like the child who squeezes his pet all the harder when he actually fears it a little, I proclaimed to the customers standing at the bar my drunken, bungling theories of art.

A comic strip artist, and at that an unknown one, knowing no great joys nor, for that matter, any great sorrows. I craved desperately some great savage joy, no matter how immense the suffering that might ensue, but my only actual pleasure was to engage in meaningless chatter with the customers and to drink their liquor.

Close to a year had gone by since I took up this debased life in the bar in Kyobashi. My cartoons were no longer confined to the children's magazines, but now appeared also in the cheap, pornographic magazines that are sold in railway stations. Under a silly pseudonym I drew dirty pictures of naked women to which I usually appended appropriate verses from the *Rubaiyat*.

Waste not your Hour, nor in the vain pursuit
Of This and That endeavour and dispute;

*Better be merry with the fruitful Grape
Than sadden after none, or bitter, Fruit.*

*Some for the Glories of This World; and some
Sigh for the Prophet's Paradise to come;
    Ah, take the Cash, and let the Promise go,
Nor heed the music of a distant Drum!*

*And that inverted Bowl we call The Sky
Whereunder crawling coop'd we live and die
    Lift not your hands to It for help—for It
As impotently rolls as you or I.*

There was at this period in my life a maiden who
pleaded with me to give up drink. "You can't go on,
drinking every day from morning to night that way."

She was a girl of seventeen or so who worked in
a little tobacco shop across the way from the bar.
Yoshiko—that was her name—was a pale girl with
crooked teeth. Whenever I went to buy cigarettes she
would smile and repeat her advice.

"What's wrong with drinking? Why is it bad?
'Better be merry with the fruitful Grape than sadden
after none, or bitter, Fruit.' Many years ago there was
a Persian . . . no, let's skip it. 'Oh, plagued no more
with Human or Divine, To-morrow's tangle to itself
resign: And lose your fingers in the tresses of The

Cypress-slender Minister of Wine.' Do you understand?"

"No, I don't."

"What a stupid little girl you are. I'm going to kiss you."

"Go ahead." She pouted out her lower lip, not in the least abashed.

"You silly fool. You and your ideas of chastity. . . ."

There was something unmistakable in Yoshiko's expression which marked her as a virgin who had never been defiled.

Soon after New Year, one night in the dead of winter, I drunkenly staggered out in the cold to buy some cigarettes and fell into a manhole in front of her shop. I shouted for Yoshiko to come save me. She hauled me out and bandaged my bruised right arm. Yoshiko, earnest and unsmiling, said, "You drink too much."

The thought of dying has never bothered me, but getting hurt, losing blood, becoming crippled and the like—no thanks. I thought as I watched Yoshiko bandage my hand that I might cut down on my drinking.

"I'm giving it up. From tomorrow on I won't touch a drop."

"Do you mean it?"

"There's no doubt about it. I'll give it up. If I give it up, will you marry me, Yoshiko?"

Asking her to marry me was, however, intended only as a joke.

"Natch."

("Natch" for "naturally" was popular at the time.)

"Right. Let's hook fingers on that. I promise I'll give it up."

The next day, as might have been expected, I spent drinking.

Towards evening I made my way to Yoshiko's shop on shaking legs and called to her. "Yoshiko, I'm sorry. I got drunk."

"Oh, you're awful. Trying to fool me by pretending to be drunk."

I was startled. I felt suddenly quite sober.

"No, it's the truth. I really have been drinking. I'm not pretending."

"Don't tease me. You're mean." She suspected nothing.

"I should think you could tell by just looking at me. I've been drinking today since noon. Forgive me."

"You're a good actor."

"I'm not acting, you little idiot. I'm going to kiss you."

"Go ahead."

"No, I'm not qualified. I'm afraid I'll have to give up the idea of marrying you. Look at my face. Red, isn't it? I've been drinking."

"It's just the sunset shining on it. Don't try to fool me. You promised yesterday you wouldn't drink. You wouldn't break a promise, would you? We hooked fingers. Don't tell me you've been drinking. It's a lie—I know it is."

Yoshiko's pale face was smiling as she sat there inside the dimly lit shop. What a holy thing uncorrupted virginity is, I thought. I had never slept with a virgin, a girl younger than myself. I'd marry her. I wanted once in my lifetime to know that great savage joy, no matter how immense the suffering that might ensue. I had always imagined that the beauty of virginity was nothing more than the sweet, sentimental illusion of stupid poets, but it really is alive and present in this world. We would get married. In the spring we'd go together on bicycles to see waterfalls framed in green leaves.

I made up my mind on the spot: it was a then-and-there decision, and I did not hesitate to steal the flower.

Not long afterwards we were married. The joy I obtained as a result of this action was not necessarily great or savage, but the suffering which ensued was staggering—so far surpassing what I had imagined that even describing it as "horrendous" would not quite cover it. The "world," after all, was still a place of bottomless horror. It was by no means a place of childlike simplicity where everything could be settled by a single then-and-there decision.

THE THIRD NOTEBOOK: PART TWO

第三の手記

二

Horiki and myself.

Despising each other as we did, we were constantly together, thereby degrading ourselves. If that is what the world calls friendship, the relations between Horiki and myself were undoubtedly those of friendship.

I threw myself on the chivalry of the madam of the bar in Kyobashi. (It is a strange use of the word

137

to speak of a woman's chivalry, but in my experience, at least in the cities, the women possessed a greater abundance of what might be termed chivalry than the men. Most men concerned themselves, all fear and trembling, only with appearances, and were stingy to boot.) She enabled me to marry Yoshiko and to rent a room on the ground floor of an apartment building near the Sumida River which we made our home. I gave up drink and devoted my energies to drawing cartoons. After dinner we would go out together to see a movie, and on the way back we would stop at a milk bar or buy pots of flowers. But more than any of these things it gave me pleasure just to listen to the words or watch the movements of my little bride, who trusted in me with all her heart. Then, just when I had begun to entertain faintly in my breast the sweet notion that perhaps there was a chance I might turn one of these days into a human being and be spared the necessity of a horrible death, Horiki showed up again.

He hailed me, "How's the great lover? Why, what's this? Do I detect a note of caution in your face—you, of all people? I've come today as a messenger from the Lady of Koenji." He lowered his voice and thrust his jaw in the direction of Yoshiko, who was preparing tea in the kitchen, as much as to ask whether it was all right to continue.

I answered nonchalantly, "It doesn't matter. You can say anything before her."

As a matter of fact, Yoshiko was what I should like to call a genius at trusting people. She suspected nothing of my relations with the madam of the bar in Kyobashi, and even after I told her all about the incident which occurred at Kamakura, she was equally unsuspicious of my relations with Tsuneko. It was not because I was an accomplished liar—at times I spoke quite bluntly, but Yoshiko seemed to take everything I said as a joke.

"You seem to be just as cocksure of yourself as ever. Anyway, it's nothing important. She asked me to tell you to visit her once in a while."

Just when I was beginning to forget, that bird of ill-omen came flapping my way, to rip open with its beak the wounds of memory. All at once shame over the past and the recollection of sin unfolded themselves before my eyes and, seized by a terror so great it made me want to shriek, I could not sit still a moment longer. "How about a drink?" I asked.

"Suits me," said Horiki.

Horiki and myself. Though outwardly he appeared to be a human being like the rest, I sometimes felt he was exactly like myself. Of course that was only after we had been making the round of the bars, drinking cheap liquor here and there. When the two of us met face to face it was as if we immediately metamorphosed into dogs of the same shape and pelt, and we bounded out through the streets covered with fallen snow.

That was how we happened to warm over, as it were, the embers of our old friendship. We went together to the bar in Kyobashi and, eventually, we two soused dogs visited Shizuko's apartment in Koenji, where I sometimes spent the night.

I shall never forget. It was a sticky hot summer's night. Horiki had come to my apartment about dusk wearing a tattered summer kimono. He told me that an emergency had come up and he had been obliged to pawn his summer suit. He asked me to lend him some money because he was anxious to redeem the suit before his aged mother found out. The matter apparently concerned him genuinely. As ill luck would have it, I hadn't any money at my place. As usual I sent Yoshiko out to the pawnshop with some of her clothes. I lent Horiki what he needed from the money she received, but there was still a little left over, and I asked Yoshiko to buy some gin with it. We went up on the roof of the apartment house, where we celebrated the evening cool with a dismal little party. Faint miasmic gusts of wind blew in from the river every now and then.

We began a guessing game of tragic and comic nouns. This game, which I myself had invented, was based on the proposition that just as nouns could be divided into masculine, feminine and neuter, so there was a distinction between tragic and comic nouns. For example, this system decreed that steamship and steam engine were both tragic nouns, while streetcar and bus were comic. Persons who failed to see why this was true were obviously unqualified to discuss art, and a playwright who included even a single tragic noun in a comedy showed himself a failure if for no other reason. The same held equally true of comic nouns in tragedies.

I began the questioning. "Are you ready? What is tobacco?"

"Tragic," Horiki answered promptly.

"What about medicine?"

"Powder or pills?"

"Injection."

"Tragic."

"I wonder. Don't forget, there are hormone injections too."

"No, there's no question but it's tragic. First of all, there's a needle—what could be more tragic than a needle?"

"You win. But, you know, medicines and doctors are, surprisingly enough, comic. What about death?"

"Comic. And that goes for Christian ministers and Buddhist priests, too."

"Bravo! Then life must be tragic?"

"Wrong. It's comic, too."

"In that case everything becomes comic. Here's one more for you. What about cartoonist? You couldn't possibly call it a comic noun, could you?"

"Tragic. An extremely tragic noun."

"What do you mean? Extremely tragic is a good description of you."

Any game which can drop to the level of such abysmal jokes is despicable, but we were very proud of what we considered to be an extremely witty diversion, never before known in the salons of the world.

I had invented one other game of a rather similar character, a guessing game of antonyms. The antonym of black is white. But the antonym of white is red. The antonym of red is black.

I asked now, "What's the antonym of flower?"

Horiki frowned in thought. "Let me see. There used to be a restaurant called the 'Flower Moon'. It must be moon."

"That's not an antonym. It's more of a synonym. Aren't star and garter synonymous? It's not an antonym."

"I've got it. It's bee."

"Bee?"

"Aren't there bees—or is it ants—in peonies?"

"What are you trying to do? No bluffing now."

"I know! Clustering clouds that cover the flowers . . ."

"You must be thinking of clouds that cover the moon."

"That's right. Wind that destroys the blossoms. It's the wind. The antonym of flower is wind."

"Pretty poor. Sounds like a line out of a popular song. You betray your origins."

"Well, then, how about something more recondite, say a mandolin?"

"Still no good. The antonym of flower . . . you're supposed to name the thing in the world which is least like a flower."

"That's what I'm trying to do. Wait! How about this—a woman?"

"Then what's a synonym for woman?"

"Entrails."

"You're not very poetic, are you? Well, then, what's the antonym for entrails?"

"Milk."

"That's pretty good. One more in that vein. Shame. What's the antonym of shame?"

"Shameless—a popular cartoonist I could name."

"What about Masao Horiki?"

By the time we reached this point we had gradually become incapable of laughter, and were beginning to experience the particular oppressiveness, as if one's head were stuffed with broken glass, that comes from getting drunk on gin.

"Don't be cheeky now. I for one have never been tied up like a common criminal the way you have."

I was taken aback. Horiki at heart did not treat me like a full human being. He could only consider me as the living corpse of a would-be suicide, a person dead to shame, an idiot ghost. His friendship had no other purpose but to utilize me in whichever way would most further his own pleasures. This thought naturally did not make me very happy, but I realized after a moment that it was entirely to be expected that Horiki should take this view of me; that from long ago, even as a child, I seemed to lack the qualifications of a human being; and that, for all I knew, contempt, even from Horiki, might be entirely merited.

I said, feigning tranquillity, "Crime. What's the antonym of crime? This is a hard one."

"The law, of course," Horiki answered flatly. I looked at his face again. Caught in the flashing red light of a neon sign on a nearby building, Horiki's face had the somber dignity of the relentless prosecutor. I felt shaken to the core.

"Crime belongs in a different category."

Imagine saying that the law was the antonym of crime! But perhaps everybody in "society" can go on living in self-satisfaction, thanks to just such simple concepts. They think that crime hatches where there are no policemen.

"Well, in that case what would it be? God? That would suit you—there's something about you that smells a little of a Christian priest. I find it offensive."

"Let's not dispose of the problem so lightly. Let's think about it a bit more together. Isn't it an interesting theme? I feel you can tell everything about a man just from his answer to this one question."

"You can't be serious. The antonym of crime is virtue. A virtuous citizen. In short, someone like myself."

"Let's not joke. Virtue is the antonym of vice, not of crime."

"Are vice and crime different?"

"They are, I think. Virtue and vice are concepts invented by human beings, words for a morality which human beings arbitrarily devised."

"What a nuisance. Well, I suppose it is God in that case. God. God. You can't go wrong if you leave everything at God . . . I'm hungry."

"Yoshiko is cooking some beans downstairs now."

"Thanks. I like beans." He lay down on the floor, his hands tucked under his head.

I said, "You don't seem to be very interested in crime."

"That's right. I'm not a criminal like you. I may indulge myself with a little dissipation, but I don't cause women to die, and I don't lift money from them either."

The voice of a resistance weak but desperate spoke from somewhere in my heart. It said that I had not caused anyone to die, that I had not lifted money from anyone—but once again the ingrained habit of considering myself evil took command.

It is quite impossible for me to contradict anyone to his face. I struggled with all my might to control the feelings which mounted more dangerously in me with each instant, the result of the depressing effects of the gin. Finally I muttered almost to myself, "Actions punishable by jail sentences are not the only crimes. If we knew the antonym of crime, I think we would know its true nature. God . . . salvation . . . love . . . light. But for God there is the antonym Satan, for salvation there is perdition, for love there is hate, for light there is darkness, for good, evil. Crime and prayer? Crime and repentance? Crime and confession? Crime and . . . no, they're all synonymous. What *is* the opposite of crime?"

"Well if you spell 'crime' backwards—no, that doesn't make sense. But the word does contain the

letters r-i-c-e. Rice. I'm hungry. Bring me something
to eat."

"Why don't you go get it yourself?" My voice
shook with a rage I had almost never before betrayed.

"All right. I'll go downstairs, then Yoshiko and
I will commit a crime together. Personal demonstra-
tion is better than empty debates. The antonym of
crime is rice. No—it's beans!" He was so drunk he
could barely articulate the words.

"Do as you please. Only get the hell out of here."

He got up mumbling incoherently. "Crime and
an empty stomach. Empty stomach and beans. No.
Those are synonyms."

Crime and punishment. Dostoievski. These words
grazed over a corner of my mind, startling me. Just
supposing Dostoievski ranged 'crime' and 'punishment' side by side not as synonyms but as antonyms.
Crime and punishment—absolutely incompatible
ideas, irreconcilable as oil and water. I felt I was
beginning to understand what lay at the bottom of
the scum-covered, turbid pond, that chaos of Dostoievski's mind—no, I still didn't quite see . . . Such
thoughts were flashing through my head like a re-
volving lantern when I heard a voice.

"Extraordinary beans you've got here. Come
have a look."

Horiki's voice and color had changed. Just a

minute before he had staggered off downstairs, and here he was back again, before I knew it.

"What is it?"

A strange excitement ran through me. The two of us went down from the roof to the second floor and were half-way down the stairs to my room on the ground floor when Horiki stopped me and whispered, "Look!" He pointed.

A small window opened over my room, through which I could see the interior. The light was lit and two animals were visible.

My eyes swam, but I murmured to myself through my violent breathing, "This is just another aspect of the behavior of human beings. There's nothing to be surprised at." I stood petrified on the staircase, not even thinking to help Yoshiko.

Horiki noisily cleared his throat. I ran back up to the roof to escape and collapsed there. The feelings which assailed me as I looked up at the summer night sky heavy with rain were not of fury or hatred, nor even of sadness. They were of overpowering fear, not the terror the sight of ghosts in a graveyard might arouse, but rather a fierce ancestral dread that could not be expressed in four or five words, something perhaps like encountering in the sacred grove of a Shinto shrine the white-clothed body of the god. My hair turned prematurely grey from that night. I had now

lost all confidence in myself, doubted all men im-
measurably, and abandoned all hopes for the things
of this world, all joy, all sympathy, eternally. This
was truly the decisive incident of my life. I had been
split through the forehead between the eyebrows, a
wound that was to throb with pain whenever I came in
contact with a human being.

"I sympathize, but I hope it's taught you a lesson.
I won't be coming back. This place is a perfect hell
... But you should forgive Yoshiko. After all, you're
not much of a prize yourself. So long." Horiki was
not stupid enough to linger in an embarrassing situation.

I got up and poured myself a glass of gin. I wept
bitterly, crying aloud. I could have wept on and on,
interminably.

Without my realizing it, Yoshiko was standing
haplessly behind me bearing a platter with a moun-
tain of beans on it. "He told me he wouldn't do anything ..."

"It's all right. Don't say anything. You didn't
know enough to distrust others. Sit down. Let's eat
the beans."

We sat down side by side and ate the beans. Is
trustfulness a sin, I wonder? The man was an illiterate
shopkeeper, an undersized runt of about thirty, who
used to ask me to draw cartoons for him, and then

would make a great ado over the trifling sums of money he paid for them.

The shopkeeper, not surprisingly, did not come again. I felt less hatred for him than I did for Horiki. Why, when he first discovered them together had he not cleared his throat then, instead of returning to the roof to inform me? On nights when I could not sleep hatred and loathing for him gathered inside me until I groaned under the pressure.

I neither forgave nor refused to forgive her. Yoshiko was a genius at trusting people. She didn't know how to suspect anyone. But the misery it caused.

God, I ask you. Is trustfulness a sin?

It was less the fact of Yoshiko's defilement than the defilement of her trust in people which became so persistent a source of grief as almost to render my life insupportable. For someone like myself in whom the ability to trust others is so cracked and broken that I am wretchedly timid and am forever trying to read the expression on people's faces, Yoshiko's immaculate trustfulness seemed clean and pure, like a waterfall among green leaves. One night sufficed to turn the waters of this pure cascade yellow and muddy. Yoshiko began from that night to fret over my every smile or frown.

She would jump when I called her, and seemed at a loss which way to turn. She remained tense and afraid, no matter how much I tried to make her smile, no matter how much I played the clown. She began to address me with an excessive profusion of honorifics.

Is immaculate trustfulness after all a source of sin?

I looked up various novels in which married women are violated. I tried reading them, but I could not find a single instance of a woman violated in so lamentable a manner as Yoshiko. Her story obviously could never be made into a novel. I might actually have felt better if anything in the least resembling love existed between that runt of a shopkeeper and Yoshiko, but one summer night Yoshiko was trusting, and that was all there was to it . . . And on account of that incident I was cleft between the eyebrows, my voice became hoarse, my hair turned prematurely grey, and Yoshiko was condemned to a life of anxiety. In most of the novels I read emphasis was placed on whether or not the husband forgave the wife's "act." It seemed to me, however, that any husband who still retains the right to forgive or not to forgive is a lucky man. If he thinks that he can't possibly forgive his wife, he ought, instead of making such a great fuss, to get divorced as quickly as possible and find a new wife. If he can't do that he should forgive and show forbearance. In either case the matter can be com-

pletely settled in whichever way the husband's feelings dictate. In other words, even though such an
incident certainly comes as a great shock to the husband, it is a shock and not an endless series of waves
which lash back at him over and over again. It seemed
to me a problem which could be disposed of by the
wrath of any husband with authority. But in our case
the husband was without authority, and when I
thought things over, I came to feel that everything
was my fault. Far from becoming enraged, I could
not utter a word of complaint; it was on account of
that rare virtue she possessed that my wife was violated, a virtue I long had prized, the unbearably piti-
ful one called immaculate trustfulness.

Is immaculate trustfulness a sin?

Now that I harbored doubts about the one virtue
I had depended on, I lost all comprehension of everything around me. My only resort was drink. My face
coarsened markedly and my teeth fell out from the
interminable drinking bouts to which I surrendered
myself. The cartoons I drew now verged on the pornographic. No, I'll come out with it plainly: I began
about this time to copy pornographic pictures which
I secretly peddled. I wanted money to buy gin. When
I looked at Yoshiko always averting her glance and
trembling, doubt gave birth to fresh doubt: it was
unlikely, wasn't it, that a woman with absolutely no

defences should have yielded only that once with the shopkeeper. Had she been also with Horiki? Or with somebody I didn't even know? I hadn't the courage to question her; writhing in my usual doubts and fears, I drank gin. Sometimes when drunk I timidly attempted a few sneaking ventures at indirect questioning. In my heart I bounded foolishly from joy to sorrow at her responses, but on the surface I never ceased my immoderate clowning. Afterwards I would inflict on Yoshiko an abominable, hellish caressing before I dropped into a dead sleep.

Towards the end of that year I came home late one night blind drunk. I felt like having a glass of sugar-water. Yoshiko seemed to be asleep, so I went myself to the kitchen to look for the sugar bowl. I took off the lid and peered inside. There was no sugar, only a thin black cardboard box. I took it absentmindedly in my hand and read the label. I was startled: somebody had scratched off most of the writing, but the part in Western letters remained intact. The word DIAL was legible.

DIAL. At the time I relied entirely on gin and never took sleeping pills. Insomnia, however, was a chronic complaint with me, and I was familiar with most sleeping pills. The contents of this one box of Dial was unquestionably more than sufficient to cause death. The seal of the box was unbroken. I must have hidden it here at some time or other in the past when I felt I might need it, after first scratching off the label. The poor child could not read Western letters, and I must have thought it was enough if I just scratched off with my nails the part of the label in Japanese. (You have committed no sin.)

I very quietly filled a glass with water, careful not to make the least noise, and deliberately broke the seal of the box. I poured the whole contents into my mouth. I calmly drained the glass of water in one gulp. I switched off the light and went to bed at once.

For three days and nights I lay as one dead. The doctor considered it an accident, and was kind enough to postpone reporting to the police. I am told that the first words I murmured as I began to recover consciousness were, "I'm going home." It's not clear even to myself what place I meant by "home," but in any case these were the words I said, accompanied, I was told, by profuse weeping.

Gradually the fog cleared, and when I regained consciousness there was Flatfish sitting at my pillow, a most unpleasant expression on his face.

"The last time was also at the end of the year, wasn't it? He always chooses the end of the year, just when everybody is frantically busy. He'll prove the death of me if he keeps on doing such things."

The madam of the bar in Kyobashi was the recipient of Flatfish's discourse.

I called, "Madam."

"What? Have you come to?" She held her smiling face directly over mine as she spoke.

I burst into tears. "Take me away from Yoshiko." The words came as a surprise even to myself.

The madam rose to her feet and breathed a barely audible sigh.

Then I made an utterly unpremeditated slip of the tongue, one so comic, so idiotic that it all but defies description. I said, "I'm going somewhere where there aren't any women."

Flatfish was the first to respond, with loud guffaws; the madam tittered; and in the midst of my tears I turned red and smiled despite myself.

"An excellent idea," said Flatfish still continuing his inane laughter. "You really ought to go to a place with no women. Everything goes wrong as soon as women are around you. Yes, a place without women is a fine suggestion."

A place without women. And the worst of it was that my delirious ravings were later to be realized in a most ghastly way.

Yoshiko seemed to have got the idea that I had swallowed the overdose of sleeping pills by way of atonement for her sin, and this made her all the more uncertain before me. She never smiled, and she looked as if she could hardly be persuaded to open her mouth. I found the apartment so oppressive that I would end by going out as usual to swill cheap liquor. After the Dial incident, however, I lost weight noticeably. My arms and legs felt heavy, and I often was too lazy to draw cartoons. Flatfish had left some money when he came to visit me. (He said, "It's a little gift from me," and offered it exactly as if it were his own money, though I gathered that it actually came from my brothers as usual. This time, unlike when I ran away from Flatfish's house, I was able to get a vague glimpse through his theatrical airs of importance; I too was clever and, pretending to be completely unaware of what was going on, humbly offered Flatfish my thanks for the money. It nevertheless gave me a strange feeling, as if at the same time I could and could not understand why people like Flatfish resorted to such complicated tricks.) I did not hesitate to use the money to go by myself to the hot springs of southern Izu. However, I am not the kind to make a leisurely tour of hot springs, and at the thought of Yoshiko I became so infinitely forlorn as to destroy completely the peaceful frame of mind which would have permitted me to gaze from my hotel window at the mountains. I did not change into sports clothes. I didn't even take the waters. Instead I would rush out into the filthy little bars that looked like souvenir stands, and drink gin until I fairly swam in it. I returned to Tokyo only sicklier for the trip.

The night I returned to Tokyo the snow was falling heavily. I drunkenly wandered along the rows of saloons behind the Ginza, singing to myself over and over again, so softly it was only a whisper, "From here it's hundreds of miles to home . . . From here it's hundreds of miles to home." I walked along kicking with the point of my shoes the snow which was accumulating. Suddenly I vomited. This was the first time I had brought up blood. It formed a big rising-sun flag in the snow. I squatted there for a while. Then with both hands I scooped up snow from places which were still clean, and washed my face. I wept.

"Where does this little path go?

Where does this little path go?"

I could hear indistinctly from the distance, like an auditory hallucination, the voice of a little girl singing. Unhappiness. There are all kinds of unhappy people in this world. I suppose it would be no exaggeration to say that the world is composed entirely of unhappy people. But those people can fight their unhappiness with society fairly and squarely, and society for its part easily understands and sympathizes with such struggles. My unhappiness stemmed entirely from my own vices, and I had no way of fighting anybody. If I had ever attempted to voice anything in the nature of a protest, even a single mumbled word, the whole of society—and not only Flatfish— would undoubtedly have cried out flabbergasted, "Imagine the audacity of him talking like that!" Am I what they call an egoist? Or am I the opposite, a man of excessively weak spirit? I really don't know myself, but since I seem in either case to be a mass of vices, I drop steadily, inevitably, into unhappiness, and I have no specific plan to stave off my descent.

I got up from the snowbank with the thought: I ought to get the proper kind of medicine without delay. I went into a pharmacy nearby. The proprietress and I exchanged looks as I entered; for that instant her eyes popped and she held her head lifted, as if caught in the light of a flash bulb. She stood ramrod stiff. But in her wide-open eyes there was no trace of alarm or dislike; her look spoke of longing, almost of the seeking for salvation. I thought, "She must be unhappy too. Unhappy people are sensitive to the unhappiness of others." Not until then did I happen to notice that she stood with difficulty, supporting herself on crutches. I suppressed a desire to run up beside her, but I could not take my eyes from her face. I felt tears starting, and saw then the tears brimming from her big eyes.

That was all. Without saying a word I went out of the pharmacy and staggered back to my apartment. I asked Yoshiko to prepare a salt solution. I drank it. I went to sleep without telling her anything. The whole of the following day I spent in bed, giving as excuse a lie to the effect that I felt a cold coming on. At night my agitation over the blood I had secretly coughed became too much for me, and I got out of bed. I went to the pharmacy again. This time I confessed with a smile to the woman what my physical condition was. In humble tones I asked her advice.

"You'll have to give up drinking."

We were like blood relatives.

"I may have alcoholic poisoning. I still want to drink."

"You musn't. My husband used to soak himself in liquor in spite of his T.B. He claimed that he killed the germs with liquor. That's how he shortened his life."

"I feel so on edge I can't stand it. I'm afraid. I'm no good for anything."

"I'll give you some medicine. But please cut out the drinking at least."

She was a widow with an only son. The boy had been attending a medical school somewhere in the provinces, but was now on leave of absence from school with the same illness that killed his father. Her father-in-law lay abed in the house with palsy. She herself had been unable to move one side of her body since she was five, when she had infantile paralysis. Hobbling here and there in the shop on her crutches she selected various medicines from the different shelves, and explained what they were.

This is a medicine to build your blood.

This is a serum for vitamin injections. Here is the hypodermic needle.

These are calcium pills. This is diastase to keep you from getting an upset stomach.

Her voice was full of tenderness as she explained each of the half-dozen medicines. The affection of this unhappy woman was however to prove too intense. At the last she said, "This is a medicine to be used when you need a drink so badly you can't stand it." She quickly wrapped the little box.

It was morphine.

She said that it was no more harmful than liquor, and I believed her. For one thing, I was just at the stage where I had come to feel the squalor of drunkenness, and I was overjoyed to be able to escape after such long bondage to the devil called alcohol. Without a flicker of hesitation I injected the morphine into my arm. My insecurity, fretfulness and timidity were swept away completely; I turned into an expansively optimistic and fluent talker. The injections made me forget how weak my body was, and I applied myself energetically to my cartoons. Sometimes I would burst out laughing even while I was drawing.

I had intended to take one shot a day, but it became two, then three; when it reached four I could no longer work unless I had my shots.

All I needed was the woman at the pharmacy to admonish me, saying how dreadful it would be if I became an addict, for me to feel that I had already become a fairly confirmed addict. (I am very susceptible to other people's suggestions. When people say to me, "You really shouldn't spend this money, but I suppose you will anyway . . ." I have the strange illusion that I would be going against expectations and somehow doing wrong unless I spent it. I invariably spend all the money immediately.) My uneasiness over having become an addict actually made me seek more of the drug.

"I beg you! One more box. I promise I'll pay you at the end of the month."

"You can pay the bill any old time as far as I'm concerned, but the police are very troublesome, you know."

Something impure, dark, reeking of the shady character always hovers about me.

"I beg you! Tell them something or other, put them off the track. I'll give you a kiss."

She blushed.

I pursued the theme. "I can't do any work unless I have the medicine. It's a kind of energy-builder for me."

"How about hormone injections?"

"Don't be silly. It's liquor or that medicine, one or the other. If I haven't got it I can't work."

"You mustn't drink."

"That's right. I haven't touched a drop of liquor since I began with that medicine. I'm in fine physical shape, thanks to you. I don't intend to go on drawing stupid cartoons forever, you know. Now that I've stopped drinking and have straightened myself out, I'm going to study. I'm sure I can become a great painter. I'll show you. If only I can get over this critical period. So, please. How about a kiss?"

She burst out laughing. "What a nuisance you are. You may already have become an addict, for all I know." Her crutches clacked as she hobbled over to the shelf to take down some medicine. "I can't give you a whole box. You'd use it all up. Here's half."

"How stingy you've become! Well, if that's the best you can do."

I gave myself a shot as soon as I got back home.

Yoshiko timidly asked, "Doesn't it hurt?"

"Of course it hurts. But I've got to do it, no

matter how painful it is. That's the only way to increase the efficiency of my work. You've noticed how healthy I've been of late." Then, playfully, "Well, to work. To work, to work."

Once, late at night, I knocked on the door of the pharmacy. As soon as I caught sight of the woman in her nightgown hobbling forward on her crutches, I threw my arms around her and kissed her. I pretended to weep.

She handed me a box without a word.

By the time I had come to realize acutely that drugs were as abominable, as foul—no, fouler—than gin, I had already become an out-and-out addict. I had truly reached the extreme of shamelessness. Out of the desire to obtain the drug I began again to make copies of pornographic pictures. I also had what might literally be called a very ugly affair with the crippled woman from the pharmacy.

I thought, "I want to die. I want to die more than ever before. There's no chance now of a recovery. No matter what sort of thing I do, no matter what I do, it's sure to be a failure, just a final coating applied to my shame. That dream of going on bicycles to see a waterfall framed in summer leaves—it was not for the likes of me. All that can happen now is that one foul, humiliating sin will be piled on another, and my sufferings will become only the more acute. I want

to die. I must die. Living itself is the source of sin."
I paced back and forth, half in a frenzy, between my
apartment and the pharmacy.

The more I worked the more morphine I consumed, and my debt at the pharmacy reached a frightening figure. Whenever the woman caught sight of
my face, the tears came to her eyes. I also wept.

Inferno.

I decided as a last resort, my last hope of escaping
the inferno, to write a long letter to my father in
which I confessed my circumstances fully and accurately (with the exception, of course, of my relations with women). If it failed I had no choice but to
hang myself, a resolve which was tantamount to a
bet on the existence of God.

The result was to make everything only the
worse: the answer, for which I waited day and night,
never came, and my anxiety and dread caused me
to increase still further the dosage of the drug.

I made up my mind one day to give myself ten
shots that night and throw myself into the river. But
on the afternoon of the very day I chose for the event,
Flatfish appeared with Horiki in tow, seemingly having managed with his diabolical intuition to sniff out
my plan.

Horiki sat in front of me and said, with a gentle
smile, the like of which I had never before seen on his

face, "I hear you've coughed blood." I felt so grateful, so happy for that gentle smile that I averted my face and wept. I was completely shattered and smothered by that one gentle smile.

I was bundled into an automobile. Flatfish informed me in a quiet tone (so calm indeed that it might almost have been characterized as compassionate) that I should have to go for the time being to a hospital, and that I should leave everything to them. Weeping helplessly, I obeyed whatever the two of them decreed, like a man bereft of all will, decision and everything else. The four of us (Yoshiko came along) were tossed in the car for quite a long time. About dusk we pulled up at the entrance to a large hospital in the woods.

My only thought was, "This must be a sanatorium."

I was given a careful, almost unpleasantly considerate examination by a young doctor. "You'll need to rest and recuperate here for a while," he said, pronouncing the words with a smile I could only describe as bashful. When Flatfish, Horiki and Yoshiko were about to go, leaving me there alone, Yoshiko handed me a bundle containing a change of clothes, then silently offered from her handbag the hypodermic needle and the remaining medicine. Is it possible she actually believed after all that it was just an energy-building medicine?

"No," I said, "I won't need it any more."

This was a really rare event. I don't think it is an exaggeration to say that it was the one and only time in my life that I refused something offered to me. My unhappiness was the unhappiness of a person who could not say no. I had been intimidated by the fear that if I declined something offered me, a yawning crevice would open between the other person's heart and myself which could never be mended through all eternity. Yet I now refused in a perfectly natural manner the morphine which I had so desperately craved. Was it because I was struck by Yoshiko's divine ignorance? I wonder if I had not already ceased at that instant to be an addict.

The young doctor with the bashful smile immediately ushered me to a ward. The key grated in the lock behind me. I was in a mental hospital.

My delirious cry after I swallowed the sleeping pills—that I would go where there were no women— had now materialized in a truly uncanny way: my ward held only male lunatics, and the nurses also were men. There was not a single woman.

I was no longer a criminal—I was a lunatic. But no, I was definitely not mad. I have never been mad for even an instant. They say, I know, that most lunatics claim the same thing. What it amounts to is that people who get put into this asylum are crazy, and those who don't are normal.

God, I ask you, is non-resistance a sin?

I had wept at that incredibly beautiful smile Horiki showed me, and forgetting both prudence and resistance, I had got into the car that took me here. And now I had become a madman. Even if released, I would be forever branded on the forehead with the word "madman," or perhaps, "reject."

Disqualified as a human being.

I had now ceased utterly to be a human being.

I came at the beginning of summer. Through the iron bars over the windows I could see water-lilies blossoming in the little pond of the hospital. Three months later, when the cosmos were beginning to bloom in the garden, my eldest brother and Flat-fish came, to my great surprise, to take me out. My brother informed me in his habitually serious, strained voice that my father had died of gastric ulcers at the end of the previous month. "We won't ask any questions about your past and we'll see to it that you have no worries as far as your living expenses are concerned. You won't have to do anything. The only thing we ask is that you leave Tokyo immediately. I know you undoubtedly have all kinds of attachments here, but we want you to begin your convalescence afresh in the country." He added that I need not worry about my various commitments in Tokyo. Flatfish would take care of them.

I felt as though I could see before my eyes the mountains and rivers back home. I nodded faintly.

A reject, exactly.

The news of my father's death eviscerated me. He was dead, that familiar, frightening presence who had never left my heart for a split second. I felt as though the vessel of my suffering had become empty, as if nothing could interest me now. I had lost even the ability to suffer.

My brother scrupulously carried out his promise. He bought a house for me at a hot spring on the coast, about four or five hours journey by rail south of the town where I grew up, an unusually warm spot for that part of Japan. The house, a thatch-covered rather ancient-looking structure, stood on the outskirts of the village. It had five rooms. The walls were peeled and the woodwork was so worm-eaten as to seem almost beyond all possibility of repair. My brother also sent to look after me an ugly woman close to sixty with horrible rusty hair.

Some three years have gone by since then. During this interval I have several times been violated in a curious manner by the old servant. Once in a while we quarrel like husband and wife. My chest ailment is sometimes better, sometimes worse; my weight fluctuates accordingly. Occasionally I cough blood. Yesterday I sent Tetsu (the old servant) off to the village drugstore to buy some sleeping pills. She came back with a box rather different in shape from the one I'm accustomed to, but I paid it no particular attention. I took ten pills before I went to bed but was surprised not to be able to sleep at all. Presently I was seized with a cramp in my stomach. I rushed to the toilet three times in succession with terrible diarrhoea. My suspicions were aroused. I examined the box of medicine carefully—it was a laxative.

As I lay on my bed staring at the ceiling, a hot water bottle on my stomach, I wondered whether I ought to complain to Tetsu.

I thought of saying, "These aren't sleeping pills. They're a laxative!" but I burst out laughing. I think "reject" must be a comic noun. I had taken a laxative in order to go to sleep.

Now I have neither happiness nor unhappiness.

Everything passes.

That is the one and only thing I have thought resembled a truth in the society of human beings where I have dwelled up to now as in a burning hell.

Everything passes.

This year I am twenty-seven. My hair has become much greyer. Most people would take me for over forty.

EPILOGUE

あとがき

I never personally met the madman who wrote these notebooks. However, I have a bare acquaintance with the woman who, as far as I can judge, figures in these notebooks as the madam of a bar in Kyobashi. She is a slightly-built, rather sickly-looking woman, with narrow, tilted eyes and a prominent nose. Something hard about her gives you the impression less of a beautiful woman than of a handsome young man. The events described in the notebooks seem to relate mainly to the Tokyo of 1930 or so, but it was not until about 1935, when the Japanese military clique was

173

first beginning to rampage in the open, that friends took me to the bar. I drank highballs there two or three times. I was never able therefore to have the pleasure of meeting the man who wrote the notebooks.

However, this February I visited a friend who was evacuated during the war to Funahashi in Chiba Prefecture. He is an acquaintance from university days, and now teaches at a woman's college. My purpose in visiting him was to ask his help in arranging the marriage of one of my relatives, but I thought while I was at it, I might buy some fresh sea food to take home to the family. I set off for Funahashi with a rucksack on my back.

Funahashi is a fairly large town facing a muddy bay. My friend had not lived there long, and even though I asked for his house by the street and number, nobody seemed able to tell me the way. It was cold, and the rucksack hurt my shoulders. Attracted by the sound of a record of violin music being played inside a coffee shop, I pushed open the door.

I vaguely remembered having seen the madam. I asked her about herself, and discovered she was in fact the madam of the bar in Kyobashi I had visited ten years before. When this was established, she professed to remember me also. We expressed exaggerated surprise and laughed a great deal. There were many things to discuss even without resorting, as people always did in those days, to questions about each other's experiences during the air raids.

I said, "You haven't changed a bit."

"No, I'm an old woman already. I creak at the joints. You're the one who really looks young."

"Don't be silly. I've got three children now. I've come today to buy them some sea food."

We exchanged these and other greetings appropriate to long-separated friends and asked for news of mutual acquaintances. The madam suddenly broke off to ask, in a rather different tone, if by chance I had ever known Yozo. I answered that I never had, whereupon she went inside and brought out three notebooks and three photographs which she handed to me. She said, "Maybe they'll make good material for a novel."

I can never write anything when people force material on me, and I was about to return the lot to her without even examining it. The photographs, however, fascinated me, and I decided after all to accept the notebooks. I promised to stop by again on the way back, and asked her if she happened to know where my friend lived. As a fellow newcomer, she knew him. Sometimes, in fact, he even patronized her shop. His house was just a few steps away.

That night after drinking for a while with my friend I decided to spend the night. I became so im-

mersed in reading the notebooks that I didn't sleep
a wink till morning.

The events described took place years ago, but I
felt sure that people today would still be quite interested in them. I thought that it would make more
sense if I asked some magazine to publish the whole
thing as it was, rather than attempt any clumsy im-
provements.

The only souvenirs of the town I could get for
my children were some dried fish. I left my friend's
house with my rucksack still half-empty, and stopped
by the coffee shop.

I came to the point at once. "I wonder if I could
borrow these notebooks for a while."

"Yes, of course."

"Is the man who wrote them still alive?"

"I haven't any idea. About ten years ago somebody sent me a parcel containing the notebooks and
the photographs to my place in Kyobashi. I'm sure
it was Yozo who sent it, but he didn't write his address
or even his name on the parcel. It got mixed up with
other things during the air raids, but miraculously
enough the notebooks were saved. Just the other day
I read through them for the first time."

"Did you cry?"

"No. I didn't cry . . . I just kept thinking that
when human beings get that way, they're no good for
anything."

"It's been ten years. I suppose he may be dead already. He must have sent the notebooks to you by way of thanks. Some parts are rather exaggerated I can tell, but you obviously suffered a hell of a lot at his hands. If everything written in these notebooks is true, I probably would have wanted to put him in an insane asylum myself if I were his friend."

"It's his father's fault," she said unemotionally. "The Yozo we knew was so easy-going and amusing, and if only he hadn't drunk—no, even though he did drink—he was a good boy, an angel."

New Directions Paperbooks — a partial listing

*BILINGUAL EDITION

For a complete listing, request a free catalog from New Directions, 80 8th Avenue, New York, NY 10011
or visit us online at **ndbooks.com**